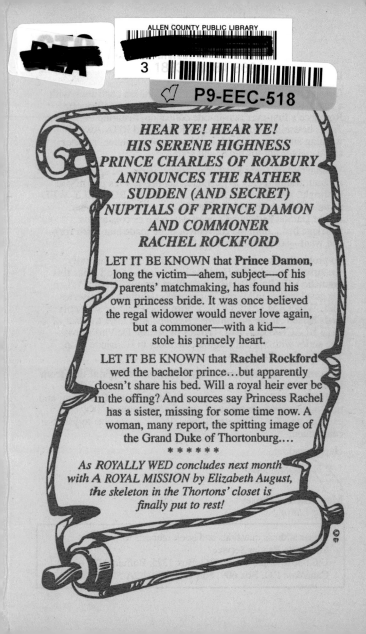

HEAR YE! HEAR YE!
HIS SERENE HIGHNESS
PRINCE CHARLES OF ROXBURY
ANNOUNCES THE RATHER
SUDDEN (AND SECRET)
NUPTIALS OF PRINCE DAMON
AND COMMONER
RACHEL ROCKFORD

LET IT BE KNOWN that **Prince Damon**,
long the victim—ahem, subject—of his
parents' matchmaking, has found his
own princess bride. It was once believed
the regal widower would never love again,
but a commoner—with a kid—
stole his princely heart.

LET IT BE KNOWN that **Rachel Rockford**
wed the bachelor prince…but apparently
doesn't share his bed. Will a royal heir ever be
in the offing? And sources say Princess Rachel
has a sister, missing for some time now. A
woman, many report, the spitting image of
the Grand Duke of Thortonburg….

* * * * * *

As ROYALLY WED concludes next month
with A ROYAL MISSION by Elizabeth August,
the skeleton in the Thortons' closet is
finally put to rest!

Dear Reader,

Our yearlong twentieth anniversary celebration continues with a spectacular lineup, starting with *Carried Away*, Silhouette Romance's first-ever two-in-one collection, featuring *New York Times* bestselling author Kasey Michaels and RITA Award-winning author Joan Hohl. In this engaging volume, mother and daughter fall for father and son!

Veteran author Tracy Sinclair provides sparks and spice as an aunt, wanting only to guarantee her nephew his privileged birthright, agrees to wed *An Eligible Stranger*. ROYALLY WED resumes with *A Royal Marriage* by rising star Cara Colter. Prince Damon Montague's heart was once as cold as his marriage bed...until his convenient bride made him wish for—and want—so much more....

To protect his ward, a gentleman guardian decides his only recourse is to make her *His Wild Young Bride*. Don't miss this dramatic VIRGIN BRIDES story from Donna Clayton. When the gavel strikes in Myrna Mackenzie's delightful miniseries THE WEDDING AUCTION, a prim schoolteacher suddenly finds herself *At the Billionaire's Bidding*. And meet the last of THE BLACKWELL BROTHERS as Sharon De Vita's cross-line series with Special Edition concludes in Romance with *The Marriage Badge*.

Next month, look for *Mercenary's Woman*, an original title from Diana Palmer that reprises her SOLDIERS OF FORTUNE miniseries. And in coming months, look for Dixie Browning and new miniseries from many of your favorite authors. It's an exciting year for Silhouette Books, and we invite you to join the celebration!

Happy reading,

Mary-Theresa Hussey

Mary-Theresa Hussey
Senior Editor

Please address questions and book requests to:
Silhouette Reader Service
U.S.: 3010 Walden Ave., P.O. Box 1325, Buffalo, NY 14269
Canadian: P.O. Box 609, Fort Erie, Ont. L2A 5X3

A ROYAL MARRIAGE

Cara Colter

Silhouette
R O M A N C E™
Published by Silhouette Books
America's Publisher of Contemporary Romance

To Rob,
still my prince after all these years

Special thanks and acknowledgment are given to
Cara Colter for her contribution to the
Royally Wed series.

 SILHOUETTE BOOKS

ISBN 0-373-19440-4

A ROYAL MARRIAGE

Copyright © 2000 by Harlequin Books S.A.

Visit Silhouette at www.eHarlequin.com

Printed in U.S.A.

Books by Cara Colter

Silhouette Romance

Dare To Dream #491
Baby in Blue #1161
Husband in Red #1243
The Cowboy, the Baby and the Bride-to-Be #1319
Truly Daddy #1363
A Bride Worth Waiting For #1388
Weddings Do Come True #1406
A Babe in the Woods #1424
A Royal Marriage #1440

CARA COLTER

shares ten acres in the wild Kootenay region of British Columbia with the man of her dreams, three children, two horses, a cat with no tail and a golden retriever who answers best to "bad dog." She loves reading, writing and the woods in winter (no bears). She says life's delights include an automatic garage door opener and the skylight over the bed that allows her to see the stars at night.

She also says, "I have not lived a neat and tidy life, and used to envy those who did. Now I see my struggles as having given me a deep appreciation of life, and of love, which I hope I succeed in passing on through the stories that I tell."

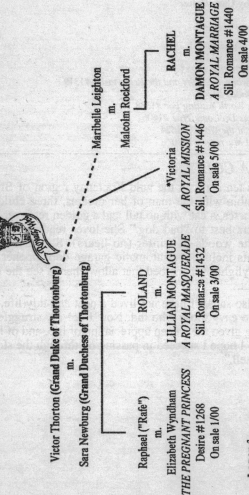

THE THORTONS

Victor Thorton (Grand Duke of Thortonburg)
m.
Sara Newburg (Grand Duchess of Thortonburg)

- - - **Maribelle Leighton**
m.
Malcolm Rockford

RAPHAEL ("Rafe")
m.
Elizabeth Wyndham
THE PREGNANT PRINCESS
Desire #1268
On sale 1/00

ROLAND
m.
Lillian Montague
A ROYAL MASQUERADE
Sil. Romance #1432
On sale 3/00

*Victoria
A ROYAL MISSION
Sil. Romance #1446
On sale 5/00

RACHEL
m.
Damon Montague
A ROYAL MARRIAGE
Sil. Romance #1440
On sale 4/00

Legend:
- - - Affair
* Child of Affair

Chapter One

"And I think she's—"

"Excuse me, miss." The bland-faced young police officer behind the counter picked up an incessantly ringing phone. "A brawl? At where? Sorry, I can't hear you. Yes. Yes..."

Rachel Rockford listened, and bit back a sigh of frustration. There was boredom and impatience in his voice. How could she possibly make him understand that this was important? *Urgent?*

"McAllistar's Pub? On Fourth, is it?"

She tucked a stray strand of her shoulder-length auburn hair behind an ear, and looked over his broad, uniformed shoulder at the police office. She found it a depressing place. The lights were too harsh, the walls too white, the desk and chairs old and scarred. Stacks of paper leaned in drunken piles off the desk. A big bulletin board behind that desk featured posters of wanted men and missing children. Incongruously, a colorful ad, featuring two people dipping in silhouette, heralded the upcoming Policeman's Ball.

No wonder the young police officer seemed so indifferent to what she was trying to tell him. He lived in a world she probably didn't even want to think about.

"He said *that?* Well, it's little wonder a fight started then."

Rachel turned from the counter, gathering her thoughts. Absently she tightened the belt of her navy blue trench coat, chosen, along with a mid-length full white skirt, to make her appear respectable, someone to be taken seriously. It didn't appear to have worked. So that left her with words. She rehearsed them in her mind, putting together the sentences that would *make* him understand.

This outer room of the precinct was every bit as bleak as what was behind the counter. Vinyl chairs, the color of pea soup, had been repaired with electrical tape. The tile floors were scuffed, the pattern long since faded. The walls were badly in need of fresh paint.

Her eyes rested on a man, in worn work clothes, slumped in one of the chairs. He was studying the grooves of his palms as if he could see his future written there and what he saw was not good. He looked as though whatever his complaint was, he had not received any satisfaction.

Rachel had a panicky sensation of wanting out of here. She did not want to be relegated to one of those chairs. She took a deep and steadying breath, prayed for patience. She must make a report about Victoria.

The constable hung up the phone. Just as she turned back to him, it began to ring again.

"Friday night," he explained, somewhat unapologetically. He picked up the phone.

She actually had to turn away again and swallow a scream of utter frustration. The last thing she wanted was to appear hysterical. She closed her eyes and counted to ten, and when she opened her eyes a man was coming up the wide outer precinct steps. A man who did not belong here.

She had dressed to be respected, to be heard, and though he had done no such thing, would not have even given such a matter a thought, she knew this man would be given what she had come here for.

Full attention. Respect. Yes, even deference.

There was something in the way he carried himself that would command all that. Something that went far beyond the obvious expense of the knee-length black overcoat, the white silk scarf draped carelessly under the collar, the gloved hands.

It was something more than his substantial height, the breadth of his shoulders, and impeccably groomed brown hair that shone like silk under the harsh precinct lights.

It was in the cut of his features, whatever that ''something'' was. He was not handsome in the traditional sense of the word. His features were too strong for that. His cheekbones, in particular, were high and prominent. His nose straight, his chin jutting.

If it was arrogance she saw in him, she might have resented the fact that he was going to get what she was not—the undivided attention of the man behind the counter. But it was not arrogance, but rather a self-confidence that went to the bone, that radiated outward as he opened the door and came through it with a masculine kind of grace and strength that was entirely without self-consciousness.

His eyes swept the precinct, pausing for a moment on the man who sat in the chair, then coming to rest on her. She found his eyes the most astonishing color.

Only hazel, Rachel admonished herself. But that didn't

quite capture all the nuances of gold and green in those eyes. He smiled briefly, a smile that lit his eyes from within and was somehow reassuring after the professional coldness of the man behind the counter. His eyes, she decided, were kind. The smile, a little upward quirk at the corner of his mouth, made her heart race unaccountably.

She turned quickly from him, reminding herself brutally about the last time she had reacted to an attractive man. Carly, twenty months old yesterday, was with the sitter now, living proof of her foolishness.

Not, she decided, that she could ever regret Carly.

The young officer hung up the phone. Anxious to get in her two cents worth before his attention was distracted by the awe-inspiring figure in the overcoat, Rachel started to speak, her rehearsed lines tumbling out. The officer held up a finger, asking her for a moment, and then pressed down the radio control in front of him and called some incomprehensible code into a large silver microphone.

"Now," he said pleasantly as if they were discussing the wonderful spring weather, "you were saying your sister is missing. When did you last see her?"

"I haven't actually *seen* her for some time," Rachel said. "But we talk on the phone from time to time, and write. I haven't been able to reach her. I *feel* like something's wrong."

"Oh," he said. "A *feeling*."

Rachel glanced over her shoulder to see if the well-dressed man was waiting impatiently for his turn at the counter. She was surprised to see he had taken a chair right next to the desolate-looking chap in the work clothes, and was talking to him in a low tone.

A lawyer, then, she thought. But the lines of his face had softened with unmistakable compassion. Surely one who dealt with human tragedy all the time would not be able to manage that. The young man in front of her seemed a perfect example. Still, the compassion on that attractive stranger's face was like a ray of light in this bleak place, and it gave her the courage to go on. She turned back to the counter as the man in the dark overcoat was sliding a cell phone from his inner pocket.

"I've written her," Rachel said. "I've been trying to call her for weeks. I came back to Thortonburg to see why I couldn't get in touch with her, and she's not at her apartment. The papers were all stacked on her porch, her mail was overflowing out of her box. A neighbor came by to collect them and said she thought Victoria was due home last week."

"Due home? So she has been away? Did you know about that?"

"Actually, I didn't, but—"

"Your sister is probably just having a good time somewhere and extended her holiday. Isn't that a possibility?"

"Why isn't it a possibility that I'm right and she's missing?" Rachel asked with a bit of heat. Still, that was exactly what her father had said when she had talked to him about her concerns. That he vaguely recalled Victoria saying she was going on holiday.

"What would make you think she's missing? I mean, besides your feeling?"

"Rachel? Is that you?"

Rachel's heart fell. Though her father had suggested if she had to be silly enough to report her sister's supposed disappearance, she should go to Lloyd Crenshaw, his old pal in the police department, she had resisted the idea. But there was Lloyd, having come through an outer door directly into the office. The papers on the desk tilted more dramatically, but did not topple, as he bulldozed by them.

A bulldozer, she thought. He had always reminded her of a bulldozer, and the police uniform did nothing at all to improve his short, squat stature.

"Lloyd," she said weakly, trying to hide the fact that he was the one person she hadn't wanted to see. "How are you?"

"Fine. My, if you don't look just the same! I thought you might have thickened up a bit. You know, with the baby and all."

Rachel smiled tightly. Lloyd Crenshaw and her father had been friends for as long as she could remember. Still, she had resisted the idea of making a report to him, not just because Lloyd had always made her uneasy, but because Victoria had always detested him.

"Are you going to look after this?" the young constable asked, making no attempt to hide his eagerness to be free of her and her intuitions.

"Look after what exactly? You don't have a problem, do you, my dear Rachel? Surely you just got home!"

There seemed to be something fake about his joviality, but then there had always been something a bit fake about him. A smile that touched his lips, but never quite made it to his crafty little brown eyes.

Out of the corner of her eye, she saw that the well-dressed man was now beside her at the counter.

"My sister is missing," she told Crenshaw. She could hear the strain in her own voice.

"Sir?" she overheard the young constable. "How may I help you?" His tone, as she had known it would be, was brimming with both deference and eagerness to be of service.

"Good evening," the man said. His voice was deep and pleasing, the confidence he exuded appearing again in his tone. "My name is Damon Montague."

He spoke softly, but Rachel lost Lloyd Crenshaw's attention immediately. His gaze swiveled to the taller man. "*Prince* Damon Montague?" he asked.

"That's correct." He nodded briefly at Crenshaw, and then looked back to the young constable. "I've had a slight problem. My—"

"A problem, sir?" Crenshaw asked. "We'll get on it right away. Let me get the report form and—"

"Please." A gloved hand was raised, and Rachel found herself once again caught in the light of those eyes. They held both apology and sympathy, and his glance told her he found Crenshaw's obsequiousness amusing.

Rachel, how can you see all that in a glance? she chastised herself.

"I couldn't help but overhear the young lady's sister is missing. She seems to be feeling some distress. I think that warrants your attention far more than an antenna broken off my vehicle. Constable—" he squinted at the young man's name tag "—Constable Burke looks more than capable of taking my complaint."

"Yes sir," Constable Burke said with such enthusiasm, Rachel felt a strong desire to smack him.

"So, your sister is missing? Victoria?" Crenshaw said loudly, turning back to her with a great show of concern that was, she suspected cynically, more for *Prince* Montague's benefit than hers. "What makes you think that? Your father hasn't mentioned it to me."

"He's never exactly made Victoria one of his priorities," Rachel said. Certainly not when they were children, so why would he bother now?

"Don't be silly. He always loved you both madly."

She took a deep breath. She had not come here to be called silly, or to be mocked for her feelings. Though Lloyd Crenshaw and her father had been friends, no one could ever say with such certainty what went on in another's home, behind closed doors. And behind closed doors, her father had been hostile to her sister, a fact that had caused Rachel to feel bewildered and guilty and caught in the middle because he had favored her so markedly.

"In fact, now that I think about it, I'm sure your father said Vicky was going away on a holiday."

Another thing her sister detested was being called Vicky.

"I think there's something wrong," Rachel said. "*Victoria* usually tells me when she's going away. Her neighbor said she had gone away, but that she should have been back by now. I'm telling you, my sister is missing."

She was not happy that the last came out with a squeak that showed how very close to tears she was.

"What would you like me to do then, dear?"

"Whatever it is you usually do when someone goes missing," she said, her voice raw.

"Well, if you insist then, we'll do a missing person's report, but really, Rachel, Vicky has always been a bit of a wild one."

She stared at him, flabbergasted. She could feel tears of frustration and fear building pressure behind her eyes. Her sister was not "wild." Not in the least. Headstrong, yes. Adventurous, maybe. Spirited, definitely.

But wild, and all the things that implied?

"She is not!" she snapped with such vehemence even she was taken aback. She met Crenshaw's eyes, and the flatness in them filled her with a feeling of defeat. She looked down at her trembling hands. "Please," she said, "please help me."

And help came. From the most unexpected of sources. Suddenly she felt the brush of that expensive overcoat against her shoulder, and saw a glove quickly slipped from the strong and warm hand that covered hers.

The sensation was shocking, unexpectedly delightful, like coming to a place of warmth and comfort after a long and lonely trek through the cold.

How long since anyone had offered her such a simple human gesture of support? How long since she had been touched?

Far too long. All the stresses and strains of single motherhood now seemed to be pushing from behind her eyes, too, this tenderness from a stranger breaking the dam of control she had built around her heart.

She felt the first tear slip down her cheek, and yanked her hand out from under the weight of his to brush it away.

"Really, Corporal," her defender said with annoyance.

"Sergeant," Crenshaw corrected him.

"Sergeant, I think just a little sensitivity would not be out of line here."

Crenshaw looked mutinous, like a little boy who had been reprimanded, but he dutifully took papers out of a drawer and began to fill them out. Rachel noticed his stubby fingers were nicotine-stained above the class ring he wore. She fished desperately in her pocket for a tissue. Her fingers felt a baby soother, and a crushed bonnet. Desperately, she considered blowing her nose in that, when a handkerchief was pressed into her hand.

She looked up at him. The gentle kindness in his eyes made her want to weep anew.

"Thank you," she said, and dabbed at her running nose, and eyes. The handkerchief was gloriously soft, and held a scent so powerful and compelling, she wanted to leave her nose in it forever.

"Rachel," said Crenshaw, "what is your second name? And your full street address?"

The pure monotony of being asked such routine questions as her correct street address, and Victoria's, and watching Crenshaw write them out with a painfully slow hand helped Rachel regain her composure.

"I'm fine now," she said quietly to the man beside her. She stared at the now used handkerchief, uncertain what to do with it. She certainly didn't want to return it to him in this condition.

"Keep it," he said, reading her mind.

"Thank you." Two thank-yous in two minutes. If he did not go soon, she'd end up owing her life to him. That was the game she and Victoria used to play. If one did the other a kind turn three times in a row, then the other would say jokingly, "Now I owe you my life." It was one of those funny, tender things that only they understood—their kindnesses to each other had been the life raft they both clung to in the turbulent waters of their growing up.

Prince Montague did not leave, and she was glad for that. She suspected Crenshaw's cooperative manner would disappear when he did. But he did not disappear, a fact not lost on Crenshaw, either.

"Sir, is your report completed?" Crenshaw asked pointedly.

"It is," Montague replied, deliberately not taking the point.

"We'll do everything we can to find who vandalized your vehicle. One of those Thortons, most likely. You're on their territory now." He chuckled at his own humor. "Perhaps the Duke hisself. The tabs say there's no love lost between your two families."

"I'm sure the Grand Duke of Thortonburg has a little

more to do than to follow me around breaking antennas off my vehicles," Montague said, a thread of irritation appearing in that well-modulated voice.

"Just attempting a little levity, sir," Crenshaw said. "Would be funny if it was him, wouldn't it?"

"I don't think so, particularly. Now what are you going to do for this young lady?"

"I done the report!"

"And then?"

"I'll post it, naturally."

"Perhaps it wouldn't be too much trouble for you to stop by—did you say Victoria—Victoria's place of residence and ask a few questions. Her landlady, her friends, might know something."

That mutinous expression appeared on Crenshaw's face again.

"Well?" Montague prodded, his voice so low that Rachel glanced up at him. There was no kindness in those eyes now. They were cold and hard. He was a man obviously very used to authority, to diffidence, to obedience.

And he got them now, though reluctantly. Crenshaw lowered his eyes and said, "We'll do whatever we can."

"Thank you," Montague said. He turned to her, and his eyes were warm again, sympathetic. "Now, are you all right?"

"Yes, I'm fine." But to her horror, just as she said the words she began to shake like a fall leaf in a breeze. She looked away from him, looked frantically at her watch. "Good grief, I'm late. I must go."

"You aren't driving anywhere in this condition," he informed her levelly. "I'll take you where you need to go."

"No, I couldn't. Not possibly. My car—"

"I'll have one of my staff return the car to you."

"Really, no."

"Is it because I'm a stranger to you?" he asked.

She wanted to tell him she felt as though she had known him always, especially when his voice became so gentle as it was right now. She shook her head, unable to speak.

"Don't worry," Crenshaw said, eavesdropping shamelessly. "I seen you together. If *you* turn up missing, his Royal Highness will be my primary suspect."

"I don't find that amusing," Montague snapped.

Crenshaw looked sulky. "Just trying to add a little levity, sir."

"Quit trying! Her sister is missing. I have a sister, too, whom I love dearly, whom I would lay down my life for, if I had to. I know how I would feel if she was missing, and there is absolutely nothing funny about it."

"Well, I guess I've been shown my place," Crenshaw said. A rat-like glint of malice appeared in the darkness of his eyes.

Montague ignored him and turned back to Rachel. "Please. Allow me to see you home."

"He don't have the right of *primae noctis* in Thortonburg, Rachel," Crenshaw said.

Rachel gasped at this reference to the feudal custom of the lord of the land having first union with its young maidens. Not, she thought ridiculously, that she qualified.

She watched as Montague turned slowly and deliberately back to Crenshaw. "I beg your pardon?"

"Besides, the tabs all say that the womenfolks are pretty safe since the prince's wife died. Grieving, he is. But I understand the bookies are taking odds on who your parents are going to match you up with. Sir."

Montague leaned his expensively clad elbows on the counter and leaned across it, almost casually.

But Rachel was not fooled and neither was Crenshaw who took a wary half step back.

"I told you once before I don't find you amusing. I don't often find it necessary to repeat myself," Montague said, his tone quiet but nonetheless low and lethal.

Crenshaw shot Rachel a look that somehow made this all her fault before he looked thoughtfully at his feet and said, "I've known Rachel since she was a baby. We're practically family. That's why I was kidding with her."

Rachel looked hard at him. Practically family?

"In fact, Rachel, your father said you might be wanting a job. Clerical, right? I'm pretty sure I could dig up something here for you."

How like her father, she thought, not to mention that she was a technical writer. He'd been angry when she had not followed through on her teaching degree, ignored the fact she had obtained at least a little success in her chosen field. Now he'd told Crenshaw any old clerical position would do. She didn't want to think about the fact if she did not turn up a contract soon that might be true. She hoped she would never be desperate enough to work in this bleak place.

"No thanks," she said firmly.

Crenshaw looked insulted, shot Montague one more look loaded with resentment, and then said, "Well, excuse me, Your Royal Holiness. If that's all, I have business elsewhere."

"Good," Damon Montague said evenly, not rising to the bait of being addressed with such officious incorrectness. "I thought you might." He did not turn away from the counter until Crenshaw had scuttled away, and closed the door behind himself. "How unfortunate that a man like that ends up a police officer. He needs to be reminded he has taken an oath to protect and serve, not bully and insult.''

He turned back to Rachel with a wry smile that gave lie to the lethal anger she had seen in his eyes only moments ago.

''He's always been somewhat disagreeable,'' she said.

''He said he was a family friend.''

''I think our definitions of friendship differ,'' she said. ''He was a student of my father's many years ago. My father is the headmaster at Thortonburg Academy. *They've* been friends for many years.''

He nodded, then said softly, ''Will you allow me to see you home? Please?''

It really seemed too ludicrous that Prince Damon Montague, eldest child of Prince Charles Montague of Roxbury, was begging to take her home.

It was a gift, really. A page pulled out of a fairy tale and dropped at her feet, humbly clad, no glass slippers. Only a fool would say no.

''No,'' she said. Even Cinderella had the good sense to run.

''I really can't allow you to drive in the condition you're in.''

''I'm not in bad condition!''

He laced his fingers through hers, briefly, and they both felt the trembling. Only one of them knew that she was no longer trembling out of shock and fear, but from the awakening of a heart, long left sleeping, now shaking off its slumber.

As if she'd been kissed by a prince.

You are mixing your fairy tales, Rachel, she told herself sternly.

''Do you have any authority in Thortonburg?'' she asked, hiding in her teasing note the quaking of her heart, ordering herself fiercely not to overreact to a random act of kindness from a stranger.

He laughed, and the sound of it was rich and warm, and made her very aware that her life, aside from the pure joy of Carly, had become bleak and worry-filled. At times the drudgery of working and caring for a baby, trying to stretch limited funds and even more limited time, made her feel strung as tight as a bow string about to launch an arrow.

"I don't think so. I just want to play knight to your damsel in distress. What do you say?"

No wonder this encounter was catching her so off guard. She was vulnerable. Still, she could not say no again. It had taken too much to do it the first time, used every ounce of her will power. She surrendered. "I'd like a ride home very much, Prince Montague."

"My friends call me Damon."

"I don't think we qualify as friends."

"Maybe not yet. But we will."

He said this so easily that she felt the warmth rush up her cheeks. Really, she was just a common girl. She was not spectacular to look at, nor wildly witty and outgoing. There was nothing about her that was going to interest royalty, to make him want to be her friend, even casually. She needed to remember that.

She went ahead of him. As they passed the man who still sat slumped in the chair, Prince Montague reached out a hand and squeezed that defeated shoulder for an instant. The man sat up straighter, managed a smile. Then the prince placed one hand on her shoulder. The fabric of her coat was light, and she could feel the heat from his hand, the utter strength of the man reflected in the sureness of his grip. He guided her down the steps and to the sleek black Jaguar parked at the meters right outside the police station. A white notice was tucked under the windshield wipers.

"What do you want to bet our friend lost no time in running right out here to give this to me?" he asked, slipping it into his pocket without looking at it.

She shot a worried look across the street at her little red Volkswagen. How much was a parking ticket these days? Her budget was already stretched to breaking with the move back here to Thortonburg, and the fact she had not yet found a contract. But there was no telltale white slip on her windshield.

"I should just go put some change in my meter," she said. "I—"

"Never mind," he said. "I'll look after it."

Rachel took fierce pride in her independence. In the fact she had never asked anyone for help since Carly was born. Why did it feel so good to have someone say that? They would look after it?

For once, she would swallow her foolish pride and accept. Just for tonight, she would let herself believe in the fairy tale.

"Thank you," she said. There. Three times. Now she owed him her life.

She wondered what it was like to be born into a family that had more money than several generations of them could spend. She wondered, as he held the door open for her and she slid into the deep leather luxury of the seats, what it felt like never to worry about money, to have as much to spend on a car as it would take to buy the small cottage that she dreamed of for herself and Carly. She had been squirreling away tiny amounts of cash toward that end since Carly had been born. But it suddenly occurred to her Carly could be a mother of three herself before she could save enough on her tight budget.

The car started with a rich purr that became a throaty growl as he put it in gear and pulled smoothly into traffic.

He found her utterly beautiful, the woman who sat beside him. Her hair, shoulder length, cut perfectly to frame the loveliness of her face, was a rich blend of colors that he did not think the term auburn did justice. Her eyes were the spectacular color of the purest jade. Her nose was small and neat and her mouth was sweet and vulnerable. There was a hint of stubbornness in the tilt of her chin.

She wore hardly a trace of makeup and the scent that wafted his way was clean and pure—soap, rather than perfume.

Her clothing, a navy blue trench coat over a white skirt and matching pumps, was plain and yet tasteful. Her hair was tucked behind her ears, and there were little white drops that matched the skirt attached to tiny earlobes.

Earlobes that begged a man's lips to nuzzle them.

The thought shocked Damon Montague. Sergeant Crenshaw might not have been delicate about it, but he was right. Since the death of Damon's wife just over a year ago, he'd been walking in a fog, held in the grip of a grief so deep, he was convinced it would never heal. Of course, it wasn't just the loss of his wife.

Sharon had died bearing their first child, a son. The infant, perfectly formed, a tiny, angelic replica of Sharon, had died, too.

He knew that people thought he had everything. And once that might have been true. But the fact was, tragedy had made him long to be the most ordinary of men. Because money, position, prestige—none of it could buy him out of this place he was in. A place of feelings so raw and overwhelming, he did not know what to do with them.

All his position had done was put his grief in a harsh spotlight, for viewing by the likes of Crenshaw. And now his position was making demands on him to get better. Get over it. Get on with life. Do his duty.

Even tonight, he'd come by private ferry from his island home of Roxbury to this neighboring island of Thortonburg to squire one of the many beautiful young women his well-meaning mother kept putting in his path. An unusually tall, if attractive girl, well-educated, from the best of families. Eligible, in other words.

When he'd come out of the opera to find his antenna broken, he'd felt relief, not anger. It was the perfect excuse to put the blond titan on his arm in a cab with his assistant, Phillip, and bid her adieu on the Opera Hall steps. No awkward moment when he had to try and escape kisses he had no heart for, conversation he could not stir interest in.

Other men's stations would not demand that they remarry before their hearts had fully healed. Other men would not have to endure such pressure to put their feelings aside and produce an heir.

An heir. No, he did not think so. He spent many quiet hours locked in a nursery that would never have a baby in it now, no matter what his station demanded.

A nursery where Sharon was, still. In that silent room, sunshine-yellow, white lace at the windows, teddy bears everywhere, he could see his wife, her head thrown back in laughter, her eyes bright with the excitement of the coming baby, of the future. She could have had a staff of a dozen in there painting and decorating, but there she would be, alone, in a paint smock that stretched ever tighter over the beautiful mound of her belly, paintbrush in hand, her tongue caught between her teeth as she painted the bumblebee on the end of Pooh's nose.

"Is something wrong?" the woman beside him asked softly.

He came back to the present with a jolt. "No," he lied, and then realized he had wasted an opportunity. His offer to drive her home was motivated not just by a sense of wanting to help her, but a desire to know more about her missing sister.

Just recently Damon had found Prince Roland Thorton in a most compromising position with his sister, Lillian. Roland had given him some story about his own sister, an illegitimate daughter of Victor the Grand Duke of Thortonburg, having been kidnapped. Roland had come to Roxbury to investigate, to see if the Thortons' arch enemies, the Montagues, were behind the kidnapping.

Even through his fury about Roland's behavior with Lillian, and even through the insult of being seen as a suspect, Damon had sensed the truth in Roland's story.

What kind of coincidence was it that Rachel's sister, a young woman from Thortonburg, had gone missing in the very same time frame? This small group of islands in the North Atlantic were known the world over for their lack of violent crime.

Of course, the Thortons' dilemma was top secret, and so Damon felt he couldn't come right out and ask Rachel the questions he wanted to ask her.

"Did you know that man back there?" she asked him quietly. "The one in the police station waiting room? I thought you were a lawyer at first."

A harder question than she knew. Damon did not know the man, but he had recognized his pain. If something good had come out of the terrible tragedy of his wife's death, it was this: he had become a man of compassion. He recognized pain in others, and could not walk away from it.

It made him ashamed that once he had been so full of himself that he didn't even recognize when others were hurting, let alone would have taken any steps to stop it.

"No," he said, "I didn't know him."

"He seemed very lost," she ventured.

"His son had been arrested. He didn't know what to do. He was a simple man. A coal miner."

"Oh, dear."

He didn't tell her that he had used his cell phone right there in the police station, and that his own lawyer was on his way from Roxbury to help the man. He just said, "I think it's going to be all right."

She smiled at him, and he liked her smile, and felt he wanted to make her do it often.

There it was again. That urge to help people in pain. Maybe because he was so helpless in the face of his own.

And yet Damon knew he must help, if it was within his power. He'd learned that life was too short to spend it engaged in ridiculous feuds. The whole world looked at, and up to the Thortons and the Montagues. Maybe they could use the prestige they had been born to, to do something really noble. Maybe they could become models of how to make the world a better place. Maybe they could actually earn some of that adoration and awe that was heaped on them at every turn.

Love one another.

He shook his head slightly, smiled wryly at himself.

A little more than a year ago he had been a man whose life was full—he managed the family's business interests, golfed, played polo and squash, swam. He attended elaborate dinners and balls and galas with his beautiful wife, went on glorious jaunts on their yacht to places in the sun.

What in that was about making the world a better place?

An old monk, Brother Raymond, whom Damon had begun to visit regularly since his wife and son's deaths kept telling him to look for the miracle. Kept claiming eventually there would be good coming out of this tragedy. Told him, so emphatically, with such enviable faith, that nothing, *nothing,* in God's world ever happened by accident.

Damon had not believed it.

And yet tonight, sitting with this quiet woman he did not know, he felt it for the first time. Not quite a premonition. More like a glimmer. Yes, a glimmer of his becoming a man bigger and deeper than the man he was before. And even more oddly, a glimmer that the future held promise. And hope. And that somehow both would be connected to this beautiful and shy stranger who sat with such quiet composure beside him as his car pierced the night.

Chapter Two

"This reminds me of the cottage in Snow White and the Seven Dwarfs," the prince commented as he pulled into her driveway, and his headlights glanced off the white stucco, paned windows and heavy wooden door of her tiny home.

More fairy tales, she thought, and then smiled. "You are about to meet the head dwarf," she murmured.

Rachel loved the little house she had found to rent, at such a reasonable price, just hours after arriving in Thortonburg. At one time it must have been a gardener's cottage. It was in a wonderful neighborhood of regal old mansions, large yards and towering trees. Prince Damon was right. It did look like the cozy little cottage Snow White found refuge in.

It surprised her that a man who looked so pragmatic, so in charge, so all male, would make such a whimsical reference. Surprised her, and pleased her. Carly's father, Bryan, probably would have thought Snow White was laundry detergent. Or worse, an illegal drug.

She reached for her car door handle, and then blushed when he stayed her with a hand on her sleeve, got out, came around and opened the door for her.

The gesture should have made her feel like a queen, but it didn't. It made her feel as if she was out of her league entirely.

She went up the curving, cobblestone walk in front of him, and fumbled in her purse for her key. With gentle firmness he removed the key from her grasp and inserted it in the door. Again, the old world courtesy was not something she was accustomed to.

She remembered when she had dated Bryan, he hadn't even come to the door for her. He'd sit out on his polished motor bike revving the engine and honking until she came out.

Which, of course, should have told her something.

"I'll take the car key off now, if you want," he said. "That way I can have someone return your car to you right away."

"That's really not necessary. I'll go back for it tomorrow."

"No, you won't. I persuaded you to leave it there, and I'll have it returned to you."

"Thank you then. It's the red Volkswagen Bug just across the street from where you were parked."

"I'll look after it."

She thought, wistfully, that a person could really get used to this. Being looked after. Having life unfold at the snap of fingers.

Prince Damon gave the door a slight push, and the sound of Carly's robust laughter burst out the open door. The sound never failed to make happiness curl around Rachel. She was determined that, despite the bad start of being born illegitimate, of being abandoned by her father,

her child was going to have a better upbringing than her own had been. Full of laughter, and warmth, and love.

Not the kind of childhood Rachel had, that made her so ripe for someone like Bryan. Looking for something she had never had, and yet had believed with her whole heart and soul must exist. Rachel had made the age-old error of mistaking the impostor passion for love.

Did she believe in romance anymore? Did she long for the love that seemed so genuine that others seemed to find but not her? She no longer knew.

Once burned, after all.

Besides, who had the time? The emotional energy? Carly deserved more than that. She deserved not to have daddy candidates trotted in and out of her life. The two of them could take on the world all by themselves.

She beckoned the prince into her tiny entryway, but he did not follow immediately, instead looked beyond her with something like wariness.

"You have a child?" he asked.

She thought he must have known. To her, it had sounded like Crenshaw's crude remark about her waistline had gone out over a loudspeaker.

A number of times since Carly was born, this had happened to her. A man showed unmistakable interest, until he found out she had a baby. It had made her pretty much lose interest in men, in dating. In some part of herself she realized she had decided, secretly and quietly, that she would never marry if it seemed it might take away from what she could give to Carly.

Of course, her own taste in men, if Bryan was any example, had thrown a scare into Rachel, too.

"A baby girl. She's twenty months old."

She reminded herself that Prince Damon of Roxbury's interest in her was quite different, anyway. Rescuing a damsel in distress, he had called it. She would be foolish to read any more into his interest than that. Theirs were worlds apart.

She was not a sleeping princess about to be kissed.

She was a single mom trying to do the best for her baby.

And then Carly bumped, on her padded rump, sleeper-encased feet first, down the narrow staircase, her blond curls scattered around cheeks flushed from the exertion and delight she attacked life with.

Rachel went down on one knee, and threw open wide her arms.

"Mommeee!"

Carly barreled across the floor, arms flung wide, balance precarious. She slid on the oval rag rug, tilted and then fell into Rachel's arms with such force that Rachel was nearly knocked over. Laughing, forgetting her dignified visitor, losing herself to the exuberance of her daughter's greeting, Rachel hugged Carly to her, buried her nose in the child's silky hair, rose and swung the baby around until she shrieked with delight.

She froze mid-swing. He was too still. She tucked Carly in tight and looked at him. Prince Damon Montague was ashen.

It reminded her of that moment in the car, when he had so definitely gone away, and the place where he had gone had caused him terrible sadness. "What is it?" she asked.

He shook himself, as a man coming out of a dream. Carly leaned toward him, her arms widespread, nearly wriggling out of Rachel's arms.

It was an invitation to be held that only the hardest heart would have been able to refuse. Damon hesitated, looked amazingly as though he was going to bolt. Instead, he smiled, though it looked as if it cost him.

"The head dwarf, I presume?" he said with complete composure. He did not take Carly, but leaned instead and touched her cheek with his hand. "Hello. Which one are you? Surely not Grumpy? Definitely not Sleepy. Or Doc. Or Dopey. You must be Happy."

Carly chortled at this, caught his hand and chomped on one of his fingers. He extricated his finger from her mouth with good grace. "Jaws wasn't one of the seven, was he?"

"No biting," Rachel admonished sternly. "Your Highness, my daughter, Carly."

"I really do want you to call me Damon," he said, and then he bowed, deep at the waist, which charmed Carly completely. Not to mention her mother. "The pleasure is all mine," he said.

Rachel realized that in her mind he was already Damon, that there was a feeling of having always known him that made formality between them seem stiff and ridiculous.

When he straightened, Carly regarded him solemnly for a minute, ran her plump fingers over the planes of his face, tugged his nose experimentally. Then she nodded her approval, and ordered loudly, "Down."

Rachel set her down, and Carly plummeted across the floor, arms out like a tightrope walker, always teetering on the very edge of a spill. She made it without hazard, however, to her overflowing toy basket, the contents of which she dumped unceremoniously on the floor. With a sigh, she plopped down on the floor beside her heap of treasures.

"Do you find yourself holding your breath a lot?" Damon asked.

"I think it's called motherhood. I'll be holding my breath until her eighteenth birthday." She thought of her missing sister, who was twenty-seven, and her recent worries, and added woefully, "And probably beyond."

"She's an unusually beautiful child," Damon said, watching with a small smile at the energy with which Carly's possessions were now being thrust back in the basket.

Of course he would know all the right things to say. They probably taught him that at prince training school, or wherever young royals went to learn to be gracious and courteous and sophisticated.

"Thank you."

He hesitated. "Her father?"

"The last I heard, running a ski lift in Canada."

"I'm sorry."

"I'm not. We're both better off without him." She said this with a trace of defiance. She did not want his pity. His gaze had drifted from the baby, and he was scanning her small living room with casual interest.

Though he kept his expression deliberately blank, no doubt he parked his car in a larger space.

And she knew the furnishings of the cottage were humble; most of them had come with it. But she had delighted at the cozy atmosphere she had created with a few plaid throws, jugs of dried flowers, bright paintings, small wicker baskets containing books and apples and papers, and the larger basket, the only one Carly could reach, which held her toys.

In one corner was the only thing in the room that qualified as state of the art, the computer that she did her writing on.

The sitter, the elderly lady who lived in the manor house on the property, came down the steps. A few strands of her gray hair had fallen out of her tidy bun, her glasses were askew, her sweater was tugged out of shape at the hem, and she was not looking nearly as sprightly as when she had come in the door several hours ago.

"My goodness," Mrs. Brumble said with weary graciousness, "she has *so* much energy. I've never seen a baby that age quite so energetic."

"Mrs. Brumble, was she awful?" Rachel asked, wide-eyed at her dignified landlady's disheveled appearance.

"Not awful. No, no. Demanding. Inquisitive. Into everything." The old lady paused, sighed and smiled. "Awful," she said. "But I meant it. I adore children, and I'll look after her whenever you have to be away."

"That's so kind," Rachel said, and meant it. Life since Carly seemed to have gotten somewhat harder. Bryan had made it clear he wanted no part of her life, and nothing to do with his child. And then her mother had died. And now her sister was missing.

And yet it almost seemed the harder life got, the more kind people were put in her path, as if to help her through it. Gifts from heaven.

Mrs. Brumble was squinting at Damon with interest. "My, my. Aren't you that Montague boy?"

Rachel did not think this was a very suitable way to address a *prince*, but he didn't seem to mind at all.

He grinned. "That would be me, all right. That Montague boy."

Mrs. Brumble offered her hand, and he took it in his, covered it with his other one for a brief moment, a gesture that Rachel could tell pleased Mrs. Brumble to no end. "I'm Eileen Brumble. I've had tea with your mother, Princess Nora, several times when I've been over to Roxbury. We have the Cancer Society in common. I met your lovely wife on one occasion, as well. I was so distressed by her death. Such a tragedy."

Rachel thought Damon's smile had become somewhat

fixed, but he said pleasantly enough, "I'll remember you to my mother."

Rachel realized her little old landlady moved in the same circles as him, among dukes and duchesses, marquises and earls. Perhaps the huge manor house that shared the same property as this humble cottage should have given her a clue. Imagine asking someone of that stature to baby-sit!

"Thank you! That would be a darling thing for you to do."

The entryway was too small for all of them, so Damon slipped into the living room while Mrs. Brumble got organized, and Rachel shed her jacket. Underneath, she was wearing a white sweater that matched her skirt, an outfit that had failed her at the police station, and which she felt failed her now because it was decidedly "blah," a selection an old-maid librarian might have made to wear to the church tea.

Maybe she did know life was not a fairy tale, maybe she had taken a vow of celibacy until Carly was safely grown-up, but she also knew there was not a woman alive who could be alone with an attractive man and not want to look her absolute best.

When the door finally closed behind the unlikely nanny, Rachel turned to find Damon studying a painting on her wall that suddenly struck her as tacky and cheap, not fun and bright.

Mrs. Brumble popped her head back in the door and called in a whisper that must have carried nearly to the Thorton estate, "This one's a keeper, child. Don't let him get away."

It was an embarrassing remark, but a kind one, too. It made Rachel feel as though the social barriers between them were not so important these days as they once had been—probably far larger in her mind than they were in either Damon's or Mrs. Brumble's.

The door closed again.

Since Rachel had expected Damon would drop her off and go, she stared at his big back with some vexation, and then said, "Would you like tea?"

Of course he wasn't going to want tea. He was waiting for an opportunity to say goodbye, and take his leave.

And they'd never see each other again.

Which was not a good ending for a fairy tale, but a far more realistic one for the way life really was, something she should be well-versed in by now.

Still, the thought of never seeing him again filled Rachel with an ache that felt oddly like sadness. Regardless of his station, he seemed like the rarest of finds.

A nice guy.

"I'd love some tea." He turned and looked at her, and the light in his green-gold eyes confirmed that. A nice guy. Not at all above sharing tea with a distressed woman in her humble hovel, despite the fact he must be used to grander things, and grander company.

"I'll take your coat then." He shrugged out of it, and for a moment she just stared at him with the coat suspended in the air between them.

The coat had really hidden a great deal of his masculine potency. She wasn't so sure about the nice guy definition anymore. Didn't nice guys generally have freckles and eyeglasses and arms the size of toothpicks?

But Damon Montague exuded an almost electrical sensuality. He had on a white shirt, pristine, definitely silk, but at sometime during the evening he had abandoned both the tie and jacket that must have gone with it. Now it was unbuttoned at the throat, showing enticing whorls of dark hair, and rolled up at the cuff, revealing forearms that looked powerful and sinewy.

The passionate part of her that had raised its ugly head so swiftly and powerfully in her past made its presence known again. Just when she thought she had successfully laid it to rest, there it was, that sensation of a fist tightening in her tummy, that sensation of *wanting* that made her mouth go dry, and her hands curl into the rich fabric of his coat. She yanked it out of his grasp, and spun away from him. She could feel the heat in her cheeks. She took a great deal of time arranging the coat on its hanger. Even when that was done she stayed behind the open door of her coat closet for a moment, afraid to come back out, afraid everything she was feeling would show in her face.

"This painting is quite good. Where did you get it?"

"At the thrift store," she said bluntly, shutting the closet door with a snap. There. A nice reminder of the chasms between their worlds.

"A good find," he said and then turned and regarded her solemnly. "Tell me if I'm being too personal, but is it very difficult? Being a single mother?"

"At least it's anonymous," she said.

He looked startled and then he grinned. It erased years from his face, and made him look roguish and even more handsome than before.

The fist did that thing in her stomach again.

"You're right. It's not as much fun as one might think being recognized everywhere you go, having your family's private affairs brought up for discussion by every Sergeant Crenshaw and Mrs. Brumble you meet."

His smile reappeared, boyish and charming. "On the other hand, if being royal is my biggest problem, you should come over and give me a slap for complaining."

"I don't think my life's as difficult as you imagine,"

she said with dignity. "I've enjoyed some success as a technical writer. And I've written a children's book that I have currently submitted. If that were published, it would mean a great deal of freedom for me." She found herself blushing wildly. Why on earth had she told him about the book? She hadn't told another soul in the whole world—except for Carly. She hurried on, "Of course, parts of bringing up a baby alone are hard. But parts of it are absolutely heavenly, and they far outweigh any challenges I face."

He looked at the baby, busy once again dumping the basket she had just refilled. "I don't have to ask about the heavenly part, do I?" he asked. "And the hard parts?"

"Really, I think they're the same difficulties anyone has. Never enough time or money." She realized everyone but him would have those kinds of problems. He was still looking at Carly, a look on his face she could not quite decipher.

"Do you have children?" she asked.

He looked at her shrewdly. "My wife, Sharon, was pregnant with our first child. A boy. They both died."

"Oh, Damon!" His name came off her lips as though she had always spoken it, always known him so familiarly. "I'm so terribly sorry." Still emotionally vulnerable from her visit at the police station, her eyes filled with tears again. "I shouldn't have asked."

"Quite frankly, it's refreshing when someone genuinely doesn't know. As I said, the world seems to know everything about me. Sometimes I catch a line in one of the trash papers that announces to the world something I didn't even know about myself."

"I don't read them. I don't have a television, either. I don't know one single thing about you that you don't know about yourself."

He laughed at that. "Go make tea. And then I want to ask you some questions about your sister."

She left the room and he took his cell phone out of his pocket and called Phillip to see what had become of him after he had dropped off Lady Beatrice Sheffield. He told Phillip where he was and asked him to come and get the key for Rachel's car.

When he lowered the antenna and folded up the phone, he turned back into the room and nearly fell over the plump pink-clad baby.

"You shouldn't sneak up on people," he admonished her.

She cooed at him, batted thick eyelashes over eyes the exact shade of green as her mother's. The little outfit she was wearing was fuzzy and made her look like a teddy bear.

"Quit trying to charm me," he told her. "It won't work. Some of the greatest in the world have given it their best shot."

She gurgled at this, tilted her head at him, and said, "Uppie."

"Yuppie? I think they call them something else now. And since I was born where most people want to be, I don't qualify as upwardly mobile. A few notches down would suit me most days."

"Uppie," she said again, and something dangerous was happening to her mouth. It was turning down. And the brows over her eyes were furrowing downward, too.

"Puppy?" he said. He scanned the room, saw a plush purple dog sticking out of the toy box, and strode over to it, snagged it and brought it back to her. "Puppy," he said, handing it to her.

She grabbed the dog by his long floppy ear and threw

it across the room with astonishing force. "Uppie," she shrieked.

He could hear the kettle whistling in the kitchen. Was that why Rachel wasn't coming to his rescue? How could this huge voice be coming from such a small scrap of humanity?

"Uppie!"

Maybe it was a good thing Rachel couldn't hear. She would think he was killing her daughter!

"Suppie?" he asked frantically. "You're hungry, right? Your mother can fix that for you." He began to edge his way toward the closed kitchen door. "I'll just get her."

A small fist tangled in his trouser leg.

He shook his leg a little, but the fist remained firm. As did the voice.

He bent over and tried to undo the little fingers, surprisingly powerful, one finger at a time.

Sweat was beginning to bead on his brow. He undid the fist, but it reattached itself to his shirt collar. Now he was caught in a most undignified position, anchored bent over, to a squalling baby.

Then, using his shirt collar, the baby pulled herself to standing. For a moment she looked gleeful, and then her arms began to windmill, and she staggered back a step. She pitched forward and wound surprisingly strong arms around his neck.

"Uppie."

"I'm not your uppie. Or your auntie," he told her. And then a light went on in his head. He got it, and it was so simple, he had to smile at himself for not getting it sooner. "Oh, up. Up."

The squalling stopped, but the pause was expectant.

So he had to choose. Pick her up or run to her mother for help.

He picked her up, rather than admit there was nothing in twenty-nine years of preparing to take command of a small kingdom that had prepared him, even remotely, for a few minutes alone with twenty-five or so pounds of baby.

Somehow, when picturing his own impending fatherhood, he had only pictured magical moments. Reading baby a story while Sharon held him. Having the baby lie across his chest in front of a warm fire. Kissing him in his cradle. Teaching him to ride a pony. It had not even occurred to him how much later *that* step came.

Of course, with a large staff, neither he nor Sharon would have ever had to deal with shrieking.

Never mind that rather pungent odor he now noticed was coming from Miss Adorable Pink Fluff.

It occurred to him that he and Sharon, considered golden and blessed, might have missed something very, very important.

He picked the baby up, gingerly, expecting the grief inside him would shatter like glass. Expecting he would feel the bottomless sadness that he would never hold the lively weight of his own little child in his arms.

But that was not what he felt.

Instead, he took strange comfort from the solid weight of the baby, the warmth of her—even the smell of her seemed to be making his heart feel. Not broken. Whole.

She leaned her head into his shoulder, thrust her thumb in her mouth. She pulled it out, pronounced him a good boy, and her eyes fluttered closed. In seconds, she was sleeping.

Just like that. From shrieking instructions to sleeping in the blink of an eye.

He stood there like stone, not quite sure what to do, not sure what he had done to deserve such exquisite trust, and not quite sure about the great ball of tenderness that seemed to be unfurling in the center of his chest.

He glanced down at the shining gold of her curls, at the sweep of her lashes, at the roundness of her cheeks.

She was like her mother. He guessed her hair would eventually darken to that exact shade of auburn.

She nestled into him, sighed, and blew a few little bubbles out parted lips, and he found himself relaxing. When he was positive that neither he nor she was going to break, he dared look around again, and was again amazed by how compact this space was.

How did two people live in a space so tiny?

He marveled, too, at how Rachel had managed to make it look so lovely with nothing more than her own sense of style. Nothing in the room was expensive—there was no crystal, no beautiful carpets, no priceless paintings. And yet the room seemed more warm and inviting than any he had ever been in.

With the exception of the yellow nursery at home.

A thought came into his head, so preposterous that he dismissed it.

But the kettle had stopped wailing, and the child had stopped wailing and now he could hear Rachel humming in the other room, and the thought would not be chased away.

Marry her.

It was, of course, a ridiculous notion. A spell being cast on him by the little minx who was now drooling down the front of his silk shirt.

And yet, was it so ridiculous?

His parents were putting unbelievable pressure on him to find a new partner.

He *liked* this woman as much as any they had shoved his way. In a very short time she had earned his respect. She seemed to him to be courageous, capable and kind.

And it was a chance for him to do someone a good turn. Who would be more deserving than Rachel to be given a brand-new life? One where she could have all the time and money she needed, where she could pamper this little girl to her heart's delight?

It would be a marriage in name only.

His heart was not into anything else. But his parents wouldn't know that. Or his countrymen. They would just see what they wanted to see. If he provided the beautiful bride, they would provide the fairy tale.

Rachel came back into the room with tea things on a lovely, rustic tray. She looked at him holding the sleeping baby, and shook her head wryly.

"She couldn't do that for poor Mrs. Brumble, could she?"

She set down the tea things, and took the baby from him. Her nose wrinkled. "Don't you know how to make a great first impression?" she scolded the sleeping baby. Sending a wry look his way, she disappeared through another door.

His arms felt strangely empty when Carly was gone, his chest suddenly cold where her warmth had puddled against him. Rachel came back a few minutes later, the baby still sleeping, the wonderful aroma of baby powder coming into the room with them. She set her daughter gently in a playpen on one side of the room, tucked a little blanket around her.

He wondered if that was the baby's bed, and thought of the empty crib at home, a beautiful piece of furniture not being used.

"Sit down," she said. He sat on the sofa. She eyed the

spot beside him for a moment and then, to his regret, took the chair at right angles from it. She poured tea in lovely, if mismatched, teacups. Probably from the thrift store, too.

He glanced at the sleeping baby, and was shocked to find that having just met her, he wanted things for her. No, more accurately, did *not* want certain things for her. Did not want her to grow up wearing hand-me-downs and thrift store clothes, did not want her sleeping in a playpen instead of a crib.

And there were certain things he did not want for Rachel, either. Crenshaw's offer of a job bothered him. Despite what she had said about writing, she would obviously need to get reestablished here. He did not want her to be getting up early in the morning, kissing her baby goodbye to go spend a day doing God knew what. Being at someone like Crenshaw's beck and call.

It blasted through his mind again. *Marry Rachel.*

Though, of course, there were all kinds of other things he could do if he wanted to help Rachel and Carly. He could have the crib packed up and sent to them, anonymously, along with a nice check.

Yes, that was what he would do. Very sensible.

He reminded himself sternly, when he found his eyes fastened on the fullness of Rachel's bottom lip, why he had come here.

He wondered how he could ask her delicately if she and her sister were full sisters. If they were, naturally the missing girl could not be the Grand Duke of Thortonburg's illegitimate daughter.

How to probe?

"Tell me about your sister," he suggested. "What makes you think she's missing?"

Rachel sighed, and tucked her feet under her. The floor was cold. He tried not to think of the baby playing on a cold floor. He tried not to think of Rachel opening her heating bill with dread.

"We aren't as close as we once were," she admitted. "Victoria didn't like Bryan, Carly's father, and it drove a wedge between us. Maybe even more so, when she was proved right. Still, we have always exchanged letters and calls, though maybe not as regularly as we once did. I guess I understand why the police are skeptical. It really is only a feeling I have. A feeling that something is wrong and my sister is in trouble. We've always been like that—very in tune with each other."

He listened carefully as she talked about her sister. Nothing she said indicated they were anything other than full sisters. Was it possible she might not know the truth? Because he heard unspoken threads that struck him as odd. Subtle hints in her conversation told him her father favored Rachel over Victoria, and her mother Victoria over Rachel. Why?

He asked, on a hunch, to see a picture of Victoria, and Rachel went and plucked one off the top of a bookshelf. She looked at it with a tender smile, wiped a fleck of dust off it with her sleeve before she passed it to him.

He struggled to keep his face impassive. Victoria was fire compared to Rachel's earth. She was beautiful, with cascading dark hair, and vibrant blue eyes that danced and sparkled. Her smile held a certain devilment.

Because he had just had close contact with Roland Thorton, he saw immediately the similarity. It wasn't just her coloring, either. It was the way her lips slanted upward, the way she cocked her eyebrow, the way she tilted her head. It was in the straight line of her nose and the angle of her cheekbones. Her resemblance to this island's most famous family was so striking, he wondered that people had not stopped in the streets to stare at her.

Victoria. A derivative of her true father's name? Victor Thorton, Grand Duke of Thortonburg?

These were not suspicions he wanted to share with Rachel.

Particularly since, if he was correct, it would follow that her beloved sister *was* really missing. Kidnapped.

It seemed to him there were very hard times ahead for her.

"Tell me about your father and mother," he said, wondering what kind of support system she had to fall back on.

"My mother died." Her voice caught, then she continued, "Rather recently."

And despite her obvious effort to carefully couch her words about her father, he ended up sounding like a somewhat nefarious character, a conclusion that was confirmed when she said quietly, "I hate saying this. And you'll think it's awful of me to say it about my own father. I will probably die of guilt. And yet I feel if I don't tell someone, I will burst from holding it inside."

"Rachel, tell me."

She hesitated. She gazed down at her hands, which were twined together.

And then she said in a small voice, "I think my father may have something to do with Victoria's disappearance."

He took in his breath sharply.

"Is that awful?" she asked, looking at him, her eyes pleading.

In all his life he had known no power greater than this one, ever. A woman's intuition.

But now he knew that she really was going to be alone through this. No mother. No father. No sister.

Look for the miracle Brother Raymond always told him.

The miracle. He had been brought to her just when she needed him most.

Closing his eyes, feeling as if he was about to jump off a cliff, he gathered his thoughts. He opened his eyes again and looked at her. Looked into the depth of her eyes, into her soul, and knew that this might not make any sense. That he did not really know her. That the time was much too short. That even Brother Raymond would tell him to be careful.

But his heart was telling him the right thing to do.

And it gave him the right words to say.

He leaped off the cliff. The words that were burning in his brain, forming in his heart, came tumbling off his lips.

"Rachel, will you marry me?"

And instead of feeling as though he was plummeting off that cliff, he felt oddly as though his soul had taken wing.

Chapter Three

The teacup fell from Rachel's fingers, and hot tea splattered all over her brand-new white skirt. The cup shattered on the floor. She stared down at the spreading brown stain on her skirt and the shards of china on her hardwood floor.

"How clumsy of me," she said, and gave her head a shake, looking anywhere but at his face. "I thought you said..." Her voice faded away. It was too ridiculous even to repeat what she had thought he said. Prince Damon of Roxbury would probably die laughing.

"I did say it," he said. "I'm sorry. I caught you totally off guard."

She looked at him then, and felt herself begin to tremble. Despite strictly instructing herself not to be a ninny, the trembling was in her voice when she spoke. "Y-y-you said it? Y-y-you asked m-m-me to m-m-marry you?"

"Oh, Rachel, I've upset you, and made a mess of things. Look, go and change and I'll look after the mess on the floor. I'm sure with a baby about you have to be very careful about things like that, don't you? Where's your broom? Or do you have a vacuum cleaner? That would be better.''

His concern for Carly touched her, even through the haze she was in. She wanted to press him about why he was proposing marriage to her, and at the same time she needed to have a few moments alone to collect herself.

In a daze she got up, and led him to the closet where her vacuum cleaner was kept. She left him looking at it, obviously not in the least familiar with how a vacuum cleaner worked. She glanced over her shoulder before she went up the narrow staircase to her room.

And knew it had finally happened.

Her mind had snapped.

Of course Damon Montague, *Prince of Roxbury,* was *not* standing in the center of her living room, trying to figure out how a vacuum cleaner worked. And of course, even if he was, he would not have asked her to marry him.

He glanced back at her, and smiled.

A smile brilliantly white, a smile that lit his eyes from within, a smile that seemed about as real as anything she had ever experienced in her entire life.

Minds didn't just snap, did they? They gave some warning first, and if there was one strength she had, it seemed to be a good, strong, practical mind. She had needed it all her life, with her mother being so weak, and her father and Victoria at each other's throats. She had needed it when her father had finally turned on her, telling her to get rid of *it.* Her darling baby, Carly, *it,* her pregnancy seeming to trigger some unfathomable darkness in her father when she had needed his support the most.

She reached her bedroom, at the top of the stairs, and shook her head wryly.

Her dysfunctional family history should be enough to make Damon Montague reconsider his marriage proposal.

But he already knew parts of it, and that she'd had a baby out of wedlock. It had not deterred him.

Frowning thoughtfully, she stripped off the skirt, ran cold water over it, trying not to think of the precious dollars she had spent on it. The stain looked stubborn, and she felt torn, unsure what protocol here was. Did you leave a prince waiting in your living room while you tried to get the stain out of a new skirt?

She heard the vacuum roar to life.

She had a feeling housecleaning wasn't exactly protocol, either.

She found that working on something so mundane, so normal, as trying to get a stain out of her skirt cleared her head. The strength returned to her legs and the jittering of her heart stopped. She scrubbed the skirt, wrung it out carefully and hung it over her shower bar.

Why on earth had he asked her, of all people, to marry him? He had known her less than an hour! He seemed to be the most rational of men. What on earth was going on in his head?

Flustered, she turned to her closet and looked through her meager wardrobe. There was absolutely no sense pretending to be anything other than what she was, and so she took a pair of jeans, faded, but clean and pressed, from their hanger and pulled them over the slender length of her legs and her hips.

She caught sight of herself in the floor-length mirror on the back of her bedroom door and paused. It seemed to her she still looked somewhat younger than she felt, especially in the jeans. She tucked her hair behind her ears, and looked at her face. Her eyes looked huge and her skin far too pale.

Victoria, on rainy afternoons, when they were growing up, had loved nothing more than to treat her far plainer younger sister to makeovers.

"Really, Rachel, look at these cheekbones. You *have* to show them off." Rachel would sit patiently while her sister puttered with her hair and her makeup, and she would be dutifully awed by the transformation that took place, but she never seemed able to make the same things happen that Victoria could.

Now, for the first time in her life, she wished she had paid more attention.

A woman should look absolutely glorious for her first marriage proposal, shouldn't she? Rachel sank down on her bed. It obviously wasn't that kind of proposal. He must have some sort of business arrangement in mind.

Damon wasn't the prince who had fallen instantly in love with Cinderella at the ball. He was coming from somewhere else, and the only way she was going to find where that was, was if she went back down those stairs.

The truth was, she really didn't want to know. It would be so wonderful if it could be like the fairy tales, one glimpse, one dance, and the prince knew he had found his partner, his soul mate for life.

Rachel sighed impatiently at herself. She'd already done that. The heated looks that said it all. They'd said it all, all right. They'd said, "Girl, you are going to get burned," and she had not listened.

Besides, why should all the power always be the man's? Why was what he felt all that ever counted? Why should she be so flattered by his attention and approval that she forgot to ask herself the most important question of all?

Rachel, what are you *feeling?*

She listened to the roar of her old vacuum and pictured

Damon running it. It should have made a ludicrous picture, but it did not. Because of his extreme self-confidence, she imagined he could do most things without ever appearing uncomfortable or foolish. She shivered, and tried to be pragmatic.

She told herself she hardly knew him. But then again, if actions spoke louder than words, she did know some very important things about him.

First and foremost was his kindness. It was so genuine. That darned fist closed in her stomach again, when she thought of the gold-green of his eyes, and she realized she was not going to be able to achieve objectivity.

One word came to her.

A word that made no sense, yet would not be denied. *Forever.*

The vacuum quit running. She heard its wheels rumbling across the floor as he hauled it back to the closet. Taking a deep breath, she stood up, and faced the mirror one more time.

She felt she looked plain, thin, tired, scared. More like a bedraggled and quivering puppy than a damsel in distress.

She took a deep breath, opened her door, and went down the steps toward her future.

Damon stuffed the vacuum back in the closet. He was not quite sure how she had gotten it in there. The hose part kept coiling up and leaping back out the door. It occurred to him his life experience was sadly lacking in those small things that most people found normal.

Having finally conquered the hose, he went over to the baby and peered in at her. Her rear end was stuck up in the air, and every now and then she would slurp noisily on her thumb and sigh in her sleep. The vacuum had sounded like a train about to come through the wall, and yet she slept on.

He heard a noise behind him, and turned. Rachel was coming down the stairs, slowly, her hand on the railing.

She was wearing jeans, and the sweater that had matched the skirt. At first glance she looked like a slender teenager, but there was a deeper quality to her. He noted an innate grace in the way she carried herself, the proud tilt of her head, the loveliness of her large eyes.

She looked more like a princess than any woman he had ever seen, and he had seen many women who were of royal blood. He had grown up moving in the same circles as the four beautiful Wyndham princesses.

Something wild rose up in him. It urged him to go to the bottom of the stairs and invite her to leap into his arms. He would whirl her around the room until she laughed just the way the baby had laughed with pure delight when her mother had picked her up.

He wanted to say to her, "Say yes. Just say yes to the wildest ride of all, the crazy adventure of life. Let's say yes, together."

It was a thought like none he had ever had before in his well-ordered life.

He examined it. *Wild?* Him? Damon Montague? A side of himself that bore further investigation, obviously.

He gazed up at her, and saw her eyes were huge and brilliant, and then realized that both were caused by fear. He decided now was not the time to be investigating his wild side. He could have kicked himself for being so insensitive to her.

So he stayed where he was, a room away from her, and using the same gentle voice that was so effective on the skittish colts that both he and his sister had such a passion for, he said, "Sit down. I'll get the tea."

She looked as if she was going to protest, but thought better of it. Her face was so pale that he did not think she could stand much longer. He cursed himself for that, too, awkwardly collected the tea things from her coffee table and went through the swinging door to her kitchen.

He stood in the tiniest kitchen he had ever seen. It reminded him of the galley on a yacht. He admitted to himself he didn't know how to get tea. Still, he'd brazened his way through vacuuming and he could manage this, too.

After gazing solemnly at the pot for a moment, it came to him that hot water was required, and as far as he knew the hot water tap was an infinite supply of that. He wrestled the dainty little lid off and saw, to his relief, there were still bags in there. He turned on the hot water tap, waited until it steamed, and then filled the pot. There was still milk and sugar on her tea tray, so he only needed one more tea cup. Hesitating, he opened a cupboard door.

Everything was neat and orderly, the space used to its greatest potential. The door he had opened contained dry goods, and he looked at them, feeling like a Peeping Tom. He wondered what macaroni and cheese was, what it tasted like, if she ate it because she wanted to, or had to. The thought of Rachel skimping on food filled him with a fierce and raw sense of protectiveness, and he closed the door with a snap, and opened the next one. He looked at neat rows of cheap crockery and mix-matched cups and saucers, reached in and got her a cup and saucer to replace the broken ones.

He loaded up the tray, and pushed open the door with his hip.

She was at the front door speaking to his assistant, Phillip Page. Phillip's eyes took in the small room, rested momentarily on the baby, and then came to him, balancing the tray.

His eyes widened and a lip moved fractionally upward, but he tipped his hat, and said blandly, "Good evening, sir."

Damon set down the tray, and found her car key, introduced her to Phillip, and then closed the door behind him. She looked up at him. Her face didn't look so pale. She was smiling a bit wryly. She really did look like a teenager in that outfit, slender as a young willow. If she lifted her arms over her head, he would be able to see her belly button, a thought that made his mouth go dry.

"I take it your staff is not accustomed to seeing you serve tea," she said.

"I can only be grateful he didn't arrive while I was vacuuming."

She laughed. Her head tilted back and showed him the lovely smooth column of her throat, and he actually felt the breath leave him at her sheer and unvarnished loveliness.

"Thank you for having Phillip pick up my car. When I described it to him, he said it was just like one he had many years ago."

She had found out more about Phillip in thirty seconds than he had in three years.

It seemed she could teach him a great deal about real people and real life. Things that he needed to know if he was going to be effective, responsible and compassionate when he took his father's place as leader of the small island of Roxbury.

He had a deep sense of their meeting being no accident in the universal scheme of things.

They sat down. He noticed this time she sat on the couch with him. He poured tea. She took hers immediately and cradled it in her hands, as if seeking comfort from the warmth of the cup.

He took a sip of his and his eyes nearly crossed, it was so terrible. He leaned over and took hers from her. "Never mind the tea. I confess, I made it with tap water."

"You've never made tea before," she stated, watching him.

"No."

Her closet door chose that moment to spring open, and the vacuum hose uncoiled.

"Or vacuumed." She was smiling slightly now. At close quarters he could see her front two teeth were a little bit crooked.

"No, but don't judge me too harshly, Rachel. I do have some sterling qualities."

She looked askance at him.

He thought what to tell her. Somehow he suspected his business acumen, his polo skills, his golf score were not going to impress her. He somehow needed to show her that, underneath it all, their humanity would not be so different. He needed to show her they would laugh together.

So he said, "I can juggle."

He was pleased to see a surprised and delighted light come on in her eyes, and the smile widen.

"You cannot."

"I can. Four things at once."

"Well, me, too. Just not in the air."

He laughed. "Would you like a demonstration?"

She looked worriedly at her tea cups, and said, "Not just yet. Damon, please tell me what is on your mind. Please."

"I know I took you by surprise, and I apologize. I should have thought more carefully about how to word what I wanted to say to you. But it came into my mind as a perfect solution for both of us, and though I am usually a man of some restraint, I said what was on my mind. I apologize, again, for startling you.''

She nodded, accepting his apology. ''A perfect solution for both of us? But I don't have a problem I need a solution for. Except my sister being missing.''

He was touched by that. That she did not see raising a daughter on her own as a problem.

''I do. I have a problem I need a solution for.'' He took a deep breath. ''I am required to marry. My station demands that of me. I was given a year to mourn my losses, and now I am officially expected to get over them and get on with the business of producing an heir for Roxbury.''

''Produce an heir?' she said, shocked. She blushed wildly and he thought she looked more like a teenager than ever.

Come to think of it, his own cheeks felt a little hot.

''I'm not asking *that* of you,'' he assured her hastily.

His own discomfort seemed to have coaxed that crooked-tooth little smile back onto her lips.

''How many ways are there to produce an heir?'' she asked innocently.

''I have no intention of producing an heir. I just need a wife. In name only.''

''I see. To make it look like you are doing your best to produce an heir.''

''I'm not ready for anything else,'' he admitted. He looked away from her, from the stillness of her gaze. ''I'm weary, already, of being bombarded with suitable marriage candidates and it's only begun. I don't want to replace Sharon, my son, as if they meant nothing.''

''What was his name?'' she asked softly, so softly he

knew it would be safe to look back at her. He knew what he would see in her eyes.

"We were going to call him Samuel. They both died very shortly after the birth."

"Oh, Damon," she said, "no one can dictate to you when to get over such a tragedy. You need to take your time."

"I know that. And apparently you know that. But my parents are far more rigid in the face of duty. I have been brought up to understand Roxbury first, personal matters second, *always.*"

"That is the worst reason I have ever heard for getting married," she said firmly.

He looked at her. He'd been right about the set of her chin. She did have a stubborn streak. He plunged ahead.

"My marriage to Sharon was arranged. We knew from a young age we would be marrying each other, and luckily we had a great deal of affection for each other. That affection grew into something more as time went by."

"Damon, you don't have to remarry. There are thousands of alternatives."

"Name one," he challenged her.

"All right." Her brow lowered in furious concentration and then she brightened. "Run away! Join the circus. You said you can juggle, after all."

He looked at her and smiled, but said nothing.

"You can't, can you?" she said softly, the brightness leaving her face.

"Physically, I could. Mentally, sometimes I want to. But occasionally I catch a glimpse of being part of a larger plan, and understand I am where I am meant to be, that I have a certain responsibility to the world that I cannot run away from.

"My parents know me well enough to know that I will

do my best to honor what is expected of me. They have begun to exert pressure, sometimes subtle and sometimes not so subtle. I have been introduced to an amazing number of suitable young women in the last several months.''

''I'm sure any one of them would be far more suitable than me! You met me in a police station, for heaven's sake. How do you think your parents would react to that?''

''Maybe I'll leave that part out when I introduce you to them,'' he said with good humor.

''*If* you introduce me,'' she shot back. ''Why not marry one of the others?''

''Because I'm sure their expectations would be the same as my parents.''

''In other words, they would expect the marriage to be real.''

''Yes.''

''Damon, I don't plan to marry. I have terrible taste in men, and I don't know how to have a relationship. I am going to try, always, to do what is best for my daughter.''

''Perfect,'' he said. ''Don't you see? You could give your daughter all the status and protection of a marriage without all the emotional trouble. That's why I thought it was a workable option for us both.''

''That's very businesslike of you.''

''In a way it's a business proposition. You would never want for anything, ever again. And neither would your daughter.''

''Damon, there's a little problem here. We don't know each other. I don't know you.''

''Look at me and tell me that you don't know me.''

Instead she looked away. A strong hand on her chin forced her to look back at him.

"What is it?" he asked quietly. "What do you see in me?"

"A good, decent man," she answered quietly, her eyes locked on his now. "That's what I see."

"Thank you. It's nice not to be seen as Prince Damon of Roxbury, a good catch."

"Mrs. Brumble saw that right away."

"Exactly. It's what her generation was taught to look for. Matches. Mergers. The better good of the society."

"You don't have your own life. I'm more free than you are," she realized suddenly.

"You could change that for me, Rachel."

"By marrying you," she said quietly.

He nodded. "That's correct. In name only. My parents would approve, I know. I know the whole country would love you."

But not you. "Your parents would approve? Why? Because I've already proven I can produce an heir?"

He was silent.

"Sooner or later your parents are going to want to know why this all-important heir is not coming along."

"Probably later," he said. "I don't intend to have more children, Rachel. My sister will marry, and her child can be the heir, a fact my parents will accept given time."

"What's your sister like?"

"She is a renegade and a free spirit, qualities that are endearing and annoying by turns. For all my efforts to exert my authority as a big brother and protect my little sister, I've never known Lily not to do exactly what she wants to do."

"Your sister sounds a lot like mine. Strong. Sure of herself." She heard the wistfulness in her own voice, and then said firmly, "Damon, I don't come from your world. I won't fit in."

She thought about the way she had worded that—as if she had accepted and was just bringing him face-to-face with one of the hard facts involved.

Still, she could not help but think of the life she was being offered. And of what it would mean for Carly. Only a fool would say no.

"Damon, no," she said with swift certainty.

"Please don't say no without thinking about it."

She was silent, though she knew now was the time to reiterate her refusal. But it had been too hard to say no the first time, and she did not have the will power to do it again.

"Regardless of your answer, I want you to know I'm going to do everything in my power to help you find your sister."

His power. All her life she had felt so powerless, and now he was offering her some of his. A substantial power. Not just for her, but for Carly.

Why not just say yes?

She had tried passion, once. That seemed like a perfectly poor way to find a partner. But Damon was not offering her a partnership, she reminded herself.

He was offering her a marriage in name only.

She thought of not having to find a job. Of not rushing to the mailbox every day, pinning her hopes on the dream of selling a book, a dream that might never come true. She thought of being able to be with Carly while she grew up. She thought of not having to look enviously in the shop windows at the pretty little dresses her baby wouldn't ever have.

She thought of forming a friendship with this man beside her. How much more inviting that sounded than the whirlwind relationship she had had with Bryan. Damon had already said theirs would not be a partnership of passion.

Stability, steadfastness. To a young mother who had shouldered all the responsibility herself from day one, it seemed unbelievably attractive to have a friend to lean on. For she was sure they would be friends.

"Will you think about it?"

She nodded. She could not trust herself to speak. If she was going to be a good mother to her child, did she really have a choice?

"I'll drop by tomorrow. Around ten. I'd like for us to take a trip by your sister's place and ask a few questions. I'm not convinced that Crenshaw will. And then we'll go for lunch and discuss this other matter further."

"I haven't found a regular sitter yet, and I can't ask Mrs. Brumble to baby-sit again. Not so soon."

"Baby-sit? Why wouldn't we bring Carly with us?"

She looked at him. Did he mean that? That he was prepared to include her baby in their friendship? "Bring Carly?"

"In light of what I've just asked you, don't you think I should get to know her?"

She studied him. It would seem he did intend to get to know them, not make the correct gesture to appease his parents and his countrymen and then just shove her and Carly in a corner of his castle somewhere.

"Do you live in a castle?" she whispered.

"I'm afraid so."

"Oh."

"Tomorrow at ten? I won't press you for an answer, Rachel. I promise."

"Thank you."

And then he leaned over and kissed her. On the cheek.

And it felt as if her heart would jump through the wall of her chest.

She stared at him. Could that possibly be enough for him? Did he really find her so unattractive that he could contemplate a lifetime of being married to her without having her in every sense of the word?

As soon as he kissed her cheek, he knew he had made a tactical error.

How could he contemplate a life with her in name only? How could he look every day at her huge green eyes and her little ear lobes and not want her? Have her?

He knew he should have listened to the voice of caution that had told him to hold off, wait, think things through.

Still, he had never done anything impulsively, his life mapped out for him from birth to death, and he could not regret this little detour of the heart.

Of course, she was going to say no.

What woman in her right mind would say yes?

And Damon really didn't know if he would feel relief or regret when she told him no. But until she gave him her answer he planned to enjoy every moment with her.

And so, even though caution warned him not to, after he kissed her cheek, he kissed her once, lightly on the lips.

And the sensation was headier than wine.

He looked at her, stunned. He leaped back off the couch. "Until tomorrow, Rachel." He spun away from her and got his coat out of the closet. He hung it over his arm and went out the door, letting it whisper shut behind him so as not to wake the baby.

He elected to stay in a hotel that night, and he lay awake most of the night, tossing and turning, contemplating what he had done.

* * *

A mile away, under her narrow high roof, Rachel also lay awake, wondering what to do, wondering where life was leading her. She listened to the spring rain start and fall with a steady pitter-patter on the roof.

Over and over she rehearsed no. No, no, no, no, *no*.

But when he knocked at the door in the morning and she opened it, she saw the rain had stopped, but the streets were full of mist. The mist seemed to surround him, and it was as if a single ray of light illuminated him.

And it seemed as though that was her world—a misty place, where the future seemed nebulous. And that Damon somehow could show her the way.

And then he smiled.

And the word moved from her heart, passed through her soul, detoured completely around her brain and her willpower and her common sense.

With her eyes locked on his, the word came to her lips, and came out her mouth, surprisingly strong and sure. The word was yes.

Chapter Four

Rachel could tell she had taken him totally off guard.

"Yes?" he said quietly. "Do you mean—"

"I mean I will marry you, if that's what you still want." For a moment panic seized her. Of course, it would not be what he still wanted. He had had all night to think of it. He would have changed his mind by now. Come to his senses.

Damon Montague was dressed more casually today, and yet he still exuded *presence*. He was dressed in knife-pressed navy blue slacks, with a soft gray lamb's wool sweater and a black leather pilot's jacket. The obvious expense of his outfit made her own, a denim jumper with a print blouse underneath, seem to her to be both cheap and dowdy, though she had felt so deliciously right in it only moments before when she had studied herself in her mirror.

She could smell the leather of his jacket, and longed to bury her nose in it, to avoid his eyes, the moment when he would say, "Oh, I've given it some thought and realized it's not really what I want."

Instead, she watched, fascinated, as a light came on in his eyes that took her breath away. It was followed by a smile. He looked joyous. Joyous that she, Rachel Rockford, had said yes to him! It looked as if he intended to pick her up and swing her around and shout with joy.

She took a wary step back from him, and looked away, trying furiously to keep her own composure. It would be so foolish to believe his wanting her was anything more than two people, virtual strangers really, seeing an opportunity to help each other out.

When she looked back, his eyes still smiled. She was sorry she had not given herself over to his exuberance. Still, he reached out and took her hand in his, and with his eyes locked on hers, lifted it to his lips.

"Thank you," he said quietly.

She let her hand linger at his lips for longer than was strictly necessary.

"When do you think we should—" Rachel couldn't quite bring herself to say "get married," as if it was a fragile thing that might pop like a balloon in front of her if she voiced it.

But Damon did not nurse the same fear. "I think we should get married as soon as possible," he said, and then said softly, his green-gold eyes intent on her face, "my parents will want to turn it into a state event."

"No!"

"That's what I thought."

"Could we just go off quietly and do it?" Rachel asked.

"I was hoping that would be what you wanted."

"My preference would actually be to keep it from everyone but your parents for the time being," Rachel said. "I don't want my sister, wherever she is, to read I got married in a paper. I want to tell her myself."

"I think that's a wonderful idea. I think given the pressures the press likes to put on new members of royal families, you might like a little time to prepare, rather than being thrust into the limelight right away."

"I would," Rachel said weakly. That was going to be her. The newest member of a royal family. Good grief, she did need time to adjust. Carly came and inserted herself between them, dressed in a little denim jumper of her own. She clutched his leg and he looked down at her, giving Rachel a moment to study him. His smile was warm and genuine.

She allowed herself an instant to think what this moment could have been like if they truly loved each other. Perhaps what they were doing was wrong in some way. Perhaps they would miss now, forever, that giddy moment when love declared itself, committed itself.

"This is what you really want, isn't it?" she said, her voice little more than a whisper.

"Uppie," Carly demanded.

He scooped the baby up with easy strength. "This is what I really want," he confirmed. "And you? Is it what you really want? Perhaps I should have given you more time. It's not a decision you should enter into lightly. Maybe I should have told you more thoroughly what you'll be up against, beginning with the vultures in the media." He calmly took Carly's finger out of his nose.

Strangely that gesture only confirmed what she already felt. As unexplainable as it might seem, she already knew she was doing precisely the right thing, for both her daughter and herself.

"Though Roxbury is a small kingdom, we get our share

of media interest—even me, who's only the heir apparent."

How could he refer to himself as only? She wondered at the strength of that feeling, so soon, and turned to get her jacket. She inspected the contents of her coat closet carefully, not ready to look back at him just yet, embarrassed by the strength of what she was feeling, afraid it might be transparent in her eyes.

"This one," he suggested, tapping her navy blue trench. "It looks like the sun may pop out later, but it's still kind of drizzly right now."

She got her coat, and together they squeezed Carly's uncooperative limbs into her little wool sweater. It was blue with brown bunnies on it. Rachel's mother had knitted it before she died.

When they had finished, he made Carly chuckle by planting his finger on her little knitted rabbit's white angora tail, and saying in a squeaky voice, "I promise I will never take your carrots again."

He had a different vehicle today, Rachel noticed when they arrived outside, and she almost wept for the tenderness it stirred in her when she saw he had a car seat installed in the back of the new bright red sport utility vehicle.

He inserted Carly in the seat, and after some grunting from both of them the straps were adjusted and snapped and the baby was secure. The car seat even had some toys belted to it.

"Did you run out and buy a whole new car for us?" Rachel asked. There were going to be adjustments, after all. This kind of wealth would take some getting used to.

Yes, a little voice inside her laughed—about five seconds.

"No. It's one of my family's vehicles. It seemed more appropriate for the outing."

"Oh." She spotted Phillip, across the street, in an unobtrusive sedan. "I suppose he looked after the car seat."

Damon actually blushed. "*I* picked it out actually. I hope it's suitable. Phillip is my concession to the need for security. My parents would be horrified to know how often I send him off to run errands."

Carly was ringing a bell that was on one of the car seat toys.

"And those?" Rachel asked, nodding at the toys. Carly was now ringing the bell over and over with some vigor. "Were they one of Phillip's errands?"

"Er, no. I picked those, too."

Rachel smiled. "You'll learn."

They had driven about two minutes when he sighed and pulled the car over. "Okay. Call me a quick learner." He got out of his seat and reached into the back. Over Carly's shouted protest, he took the bell off the car seat and tossed it in the front. Rachel laughed as he slid back in beside her.

"All right, no more noisy toys, ever. Which means that delightful fire engine with the working siren that I saw this morning is out of the question. Now, let's go see what we can find out about your sister. Where does she live?"

"She has a flat close to downtown." Rachel gave him instructions.

In a few minutes they pulled up outside of a large old house.

"Her flat is up the back staircase, the top floor of the house."

They made their way up the stairs. The morning paper had not been delivered, she noticed, and allowed herself to wish for a moment that maybe it had been taken in.

She peered in the window while Damon held Carly. The flat was very small, but neat and tidy. And then a shadow moved inside.

"She's in there!" Rachel squealed and rang the doorbell.

But when the door opened her heart plummeted. It was not Victoria standing in front of her, but a short brunette who was round in all the right places.

"Hello," the young woman greeted them, her eyes dismissing Rachel in a second, and her smile widening for Damon. "Are you looking for Vic?"

"I am," Rachel said. "I'm her sister, Rachel."

"And this is?" She blinked at Damon.

"I'm Damon Montague."

Rachel watched the name register on the woman's face. This was what it would be like to be with Damon, she thought. Other women were going to want him. Or would that change when they were married? She doubted it.

"I'm Heidi Ramsey, Your Highness. I've read so much about you, but of course I didn't dream I would ever meet you." She smiled coyly. "The pictures don't do you justice, really."

"Thank you." His voice was remote, a different Damon than Rachel knew, and she slid him a quick look out of the corner of her eye.

Heidi seemed to realize she had failed to impress the prince and tried a different tack. "What an adorable baby. Can I hold her?"

Rachel felt, a bit impatiently, that this show of interest in the baby was entirely for Damon's benefit. Victoria had mentioned her friend, Heidi, to her on more than one occasion. She called her The Man Magnet.

Damon glanced at Rachel, hesitated, and then handed Carly to Heidi. Heidi cooed prettily at the baby, a patently theatrical gesture intended, Rachel thought cynically, to impress the prince with her motherliness.

"Vic asked me to look after her place while she was away."

"So she is away!" Rachel said, feeling relieved, followed quickly by feeling utterly foolish. She had made a police report! Damon had taken her worries seriously!

"How long is she away for?" Damon asked smoothly, apparently not the least inclined to take her less seriously even though she might be leading him on a wild-goose chase.

"Oh, well that's the thing. Her landlady called me yesterday and told me she wasn't home yet. I've nearly killed the plants and somebody's snitched her papers and her mail because I thought she was supposed to be home a week ago. I feel bad that I didn't check, but I've got my own life."

Rachel figured the latter, aimed at Damon, was just to let him know her social calendar was full, but she could probably squeeze him in.

Rachel scolded herself for reading that much in to what Heidi had said. The fear leaped in her again. "*I* picked up the mail," she said. "When was she supposed to be back?"

"Oh, a week ago? A few days ago? I can't exactly remember. Oh, don't look so worried, love, Vic can look after herself. Besides, I called your father when I came by and saw she wasn't home yet. He's heard from her. She's been delayed on the continent."

"Don't you have a number where I can reach her?"

"Gosh. I don't. Do you want to look around? She might have left something. I know she wouldn't mind."

"Thanks. I think we will," Rachel said. She found Carly thrust into her arms. Heidi zeroed in on Damon while Rachel made her way to the kitchen at the back of the flat. She noticed that her sister had framed the baby pictures of Carly that Rachel had sent her, and that everything was neat and tidy, just the way people left things when they would be gone for a while.

The kitchen had some papers stacked on the table, and Rachel set Carly on the floor and went through them. She heard the front door close, and was suddenly aware of how she had been waiting for that sound, how she had been registering the high-pitched giggles with growing annoyance.

Jealous, she deduced with irritation. How could she be jealous over a man she didn't even know?

"Maybe you asked the wrong girl to marry you, Damon," she said, when he came into the room. "Heidi would have you in a second."

"I didn't ask the wrong girl," he said firmly, and didn't elaborate.

It occurred to her that he was quite used to having the female populace throw themselves at him and knew how to handle it with just the right combination of reserve and grace.

"Have you found anything?" he asked.

"No."

He came and looked over her shoulder. His sweater brushed her shoulder with heavenly softness. His breath stirred the tendrils of her hair. She thought he smelled wonderful.

"Those look like bills. It seems to me if your sister had been planning a really extended stay somewhere, she might have made arrangements to pay them. I can tell by the apartment she's extremely organized, likes everything in its place."

Rachel had not seen the bills in quite that light. Victoria's personal phone book hung on a chain by the phone and he unfastened it and scanned it. "She has a lot of friends," he said. "Someone will know where she is. Would it be all right with you if I gave this to Phillip? He can start making some calls."

"That's a great idea." Then she came across the receipt for the airline ticket. They studied it together.

"It's just as Heidi says," Rachel said. "She was due home awhile ago." The feeling was back, stronger than before. That something had gone terribly wrong for her sister.

He seemed to sense her inner agitation, because he touched her cheek, cupped it in the palm of his hand.

"It's going to be all right, Rachel."

"Do you think so?"

"Yes," he said firmly, "I do. I have a suggestion. Give me the receipt for the airline ticket and I'll have Phillip check that out, too. We should at least be able to find out if she was on the plane."

She looked at him, amazed by the orderly way his mind worked, so relieved that he was here with her. She felt that without his strong and calm presence beside her, she would not be coping well at all. It seemed that with saying yes to his proposal she had allowed herself to feel how very alone she had been for a long, long time.

"Let's go have some lunch," he suggested. "We'll give what we've got to Phillip and then leave this alone entirely until tomorrow. That should give the little worry line in your forehead a chance to relax. Tomorrow, I'll go with you to talk to your father."

She rubbed at the worry line. "Would you? Oh, thank you." Somehow she knew Damon was going to be able to see things about her father that she couldn't see.

"Did you want to announce our plans to him?" Damon asked softly.

"No," she said without hesitation. "I'm sorry. I wonder what kind of person you will think I am. But no."

"Rachel, when I look at you, I know what kind of person you are."

"It takes a long time to know that."

"Sometimes. Not always."

He bent his head and kissed her softly and briefly on the lips.

She stared at him wide-eyed.

He smiled. "And if I didn't know before I did that, I would certainly know now."

They heard a crash, and realized Carly had gotten away from them. They dashed into the living room to find a lamp turned on its side, thankfully nothing broken.

Nothing had ever detracted Rachel from her daughter's safety before and she felt shocked. If she was going to marry this man, and it seemed she was, she was going to have to build a big wall of defense around how she physically reacted to him.

She rubbed her lips and, though it cost her, said, "Damon, I don't think we should do that. Kiss. It will just make everything too complicated."

Something felt hollow and empty inside her as soon as she had said it.

And for the first time she saw the same face he had shown to Heidi, remote and princely. He said, "Of course. You're absolutely right."

Locking the door and pulling it shut behind them, Damon scooped up Carly and they went down the steps.

"We could walk to lunch," Rachel said. "Parking can be a problem downtown."

He smiled at this, and she realized parking had never

been a problem for him in his life. With the exception of last night, when he had gotten a ticket.

"We can walk if you want," he said.

And she did. The sun had come out, and it was only a few blocks to downtown. He tucked Carly into the crook of his arm, and held out his other one.

He meant to hold her hand, she realized. She hesitated, wondering if this wasn't somehow in the same department as kissing, but then found herself unable to resist. She took the offered hand and felt it close around hers. Nothing had ever felt so right.

Damon felt as if they were his family as they walked down the street. He was not sure when spring had ever looked so lovely to him—tiny green buds getting ready to explode from their sheaths, the scent of flowers in the air, the streets washed clean from the recent rain.

The baby felt right nestled into his chest.

And Rachel's hand felt right in his.

She had said yes. His impulse when she had said those words had been to pick her up by her waist, and lift her into the air above his head, bring her back down into the circle of his arms and dance with her on her stoop.

But he had seen her shy away almost immediately after she had answered him and so he had contained his impulses. They astonished him anyway. Made him feel like an excitable schoolboy.

She was absolutely right about the kissing. He couldn't. And yet ever since she had said he couldn't, her lips beckoned his eyes. They were soft and full and slightly moist. Her bottom lip was fuller than the top one and had the cutest little crease in the center of it. He knew what they tasted like now, those lips, faintly of strawberries, and so every time he looked at them he felt tormented.

Perhaps there was something fundamentally wrong with what he was doing, making an arrangement that amounted to pure business in the area of the heart, of emotion, where business did not belong.

Not that that was strictly true in his experience. His union with Sharon had been strictly about business—a strong alliance between two families. And it had become, in time, something more. Was he secretly hoping the same thing would happen here?

Was he being fair to her if he had a secret agenda?

He stopped this train of thought, annoyed with himself. If his agenda was secret, he had also kept it a secret from himself. He was not an emotional man and never had been. He had always made decisions based on pure reason and rational thought and he had not been let down yet.

It was true, since his personal tragedy, he was more aware of his emotional side, a softer side, but he was not going to let it *rule* him.

He deliberately set his mind in a different direction. The bills in Victoria's apartment had worried him, as had the news that she was due back a week ago, if that silly woman had her facts straight.

He found himself not looking forward to meeting Rachel's father.

But meanwhile he planned to follow his own advice and not worry. They would do what they could do, the rest they had to let go of.

Words from Brother Raymond, whom he would call about performing a wedding ceremony. Would his friend be happy for him? Or would he think Damon had lost his mind, and behaved with an impulsiveness not becoming in a man of his position? What the old friar thought mattered to him, but not enough to make him change his mind. His course was set, and he was a little surprised himself to see how unmovable he felt in his resolve.

Again, he brought himself back to the moment, the sheer contentment of having the baby riding against him, Rachel's hand in his, and the spring sunshine warming his cheeks.

They reached downtown, and he watched as they walked by shops, watched what Rachel's eyes trailed to, what held her interest, what she dismissed. He could tell her taste ran to colorful and cozy. She stopped for a moment in front of a furniture store. In the window were two blue checked love seats, with solid-colored wing chairs on the side, an antique chest in the center.

"I've always loved this arrangement," she said. "It looks like the kind of living room where people love to sit and read and visit. The kind of living room with a fireplace and an old dog on the floor."

He found he liked it, too. It was not as formal as what he was accustomed to, but the grouping created an atmosphere of warmth and coziness, just like her cottage.

They moved on to the next window of the same furniture store. In it was a big, four-poster bed, covered in white lace and mounds of pillows.

"What do you think of that?" he asked.

She blushed. "It looks like something out of a romantic dream. Not like something anyone with children could ever have."

But he saw that there was a wistful light burning deep in her green eyes.

"Any ideas for lunch?" he asked as they walked on.

She laughed. "I'm only just back here. I'm afraid the only eating establishment I'm familiar with is McDonald's."

He laughed, too, liking that about her. She was fresh

and real, and made no attempts to hide who she was or to pretend to be anything else. She was refreshingly genuine.

"I know a little place around the corner."

The little place around the corner, he could tell from the look on the maitre d's face had never seated a baby. But he was recognized and at his request a small and private alcove was cleared for their use. There were certain benefits to having a position in life, he realized as the staff, without letting on what contortions they had had to go to to find it, brought a high chair and set it up.

Rachel was studying the menu with determined concentration.

"The Red Snapper is excellent here," he said.

She looked relieved, as he had suspected she might, and immediately closed the menu.

"And what will Carly have?" he asked.

"Do they have french fries here?" Rachel whispered. "That's usually what I get for her when we go out."

Going out for them had been McDonald's. For a brief moment he wondered about the chasm he was asking her to cross.

They placed their orders, and he asked for the french fries. The waiter looked stunned, but said of course they could find french fries and then scurried away. Damon suspected a bus boy would be running to McDonald's for them within minutes.

Rachel studied the heavy silver and the linen tablecloth. Her eyes drifted to the eclectic selection of antique tables and chairs, and then to the chandelier that hung over their table. She seemed to want to look anywhere but at him, and she suddenly seemed to him to be overwhelmed and scared.

"This is the moment you've been waiting for," he told her.

"It is?" she asked, her eyes coming to his face full of question.

"It is. I'm going to juggle."

"You are not. Damon. Not in here."

"Why on earth not? There's no one here but us. This is a private little section of the restaurant."

"What if you break something?"

"Ye of little faith."

"Well, what if you do?"

"They'll throw us out," he teased her.

"You'll probably be on the front page of tomorrow morning's tabs," she said with a regal sniff. If only he could find a way to tell her that she belonged here more than he did, with that wonderful air she carried within her, with her innate grace, and the lovely and proud tilt of her chin. Didn't she know she could fit in, belong, anywhere?

He suddenly felt honored that he had been given this to teach her.

"Better to get my name in the gossip rags for this," he said, picking up a glass and testing the weight of it, "than for a lot of other things I can think of."

He was rewarded with a strangled little laugh from her. "Hand me your glass."

"Oh, Damon," she said, but she handed him the glass. He tossed one up experimentally, and caught it, and then the other.

She snorted reluctantly from trying to hold back the laughter.

Carly gave up trying to escape the confines of the high chair, and watched him with wide eyes. Her coo of delight when he began to juggle the two glasses very slowly encouraged him. He picked up speed a bit.

Rachel was really laughing now, and so was the baby, chortling happily and chewing her pudgy fists.

He juggled the two glasses, setting them down on the table a split second before the waiter returned bringing them fresh bread sticks.

"Anything else, sir?" the waiter asked.

"Two more glasses, please," Damon said, deadpan.

The waiter was carefully practiced never to show surprise or curiosity. Rachel laughed into her handkerchief. The glasses were brought immediately.

They really were an awkward shape to juggle with. Again, he put the two glasses up, and then when he had formed a rhythm he added a third. He dared not look at his audience now. Again, he established a rhythm and then added the fourth glass.

Of course, the best part was when he dropped them all.

Rachel bent over double from laughing, Carly banged her high chair and demanded more, and the glasses fell harmlessly on the thickly padded carpet.

The food came. He knew she would have been astonished to know how he enjoyed her manners which were perfect and schoolgirlish, without any kind of flourish or pretension. And, of course, Carly ate with charming vigor, spreading ketchup from her toes to her hairline with happy abandon.

After lunch, and after Carly had been cleaned up, he suggested a tour of some of the shops. He was driven by a desire to give Rachel the moon, and hoped he could start by getting her to accept a few dresses and trinkets for herself and the baby.

"I don't know," she said uneasily. He could see the pride in her face.

"Rachel, in a very short time, if things work right, and

I think they will, you will be my wife. Are you going to insist on paying room and board?"

She looked no less stubborn.

"By the time the bills come in we'll be married," he said.

"Damon, I've never taken anything from anyone. Even as a teenager, I earned most of my own money baby-sitting and such. I can't become your dependent."

"What are you suggesting? That you'll get a job after we're married? That kind of defeats the purpose from Carly's point of view, and wouldn't go over real big at the castle, truth be told."

Still, she was silent.

He took a deep breath. "Think of it as a job. I've hired you to do a job. And I'm going to pay you in things other than money. Dresses and jewelry and a lovely place to live. Can you think of it like that?"

"With difficulty."

"Rachel, you are hiding a stubborn streak under that lovely facade."

She smiled. "You might as well find out now. I wouldn't want to surprise you with it later."

"Let's go shopping. We'll just get a few things. Some basics. A ring. A dress or two. A few outfits for Carly."

He could tell it was the outfits for Carly that swayed her.

The stubbornness faded from her features, and she smiled at him. He realized he would buy her the earth to see that smile again.

He knew the better shops of Thortonburg well, as Roxbury was really too tiny to boast any kind of shopping. Thortonburg had some wonderful choices. Sharon had loved Rosalitta's in particular.

He himself had never been in Rosalitta's. He had never

shopped with a woman before, except once when he and Sharon had haunted the little antique shops she adored, looking for just the right touches for the nursery.

Rosalitta's was furnished very formally, like the rooms he was more accustomed to. In between a few tastefully displayed dresses were couches and bookshelves and coffee tables. Despite the fact he had never been in here, he was recognized instantly.

With touching shyness, hesitating, Rachel finally chose a few items to try on, and a regal member of the sales staff led them deeper into the store to the change rooms.

The deeper they went into the store, the more intimate the apparel became. Damon saw a white negligee that took his breath away when he imagined Rachel in it. Of course, he knew he would never be able to get her to agree to try that on.

The change rooms were up a little flight of stairs, a thickly carpeted alcove full of mirrors, with a few richly brocaded settees for the waiting gentlemen to sit on.

Rachel disappeared behind a mahogany door, though he was delighted to see that he could see her ankles underneath it. He told the saleslady to just keep bringing things for her to try until she told her to stop. Rachel actually began to seem to enjoy what was happening. The saleslady made a tremendous fuss over how perfectly things fit her, and Rachel showed an almost childish wonder in the array of items brought for her to try on.

For three or four minutes Carly had been content to sit on his knee.

For another three or four they had played horsey.

Now he was lying on the floor with the baby crawling all over him, and the salesladies indulgently making their way around him.

Rachel came out in a full skirt and a matching silk

sleeveless tunic. It was in jade green, the exact color of her eyes.

He watched as she turned self-consciously in front of him, and then caught her own reflection in the mirror and stood for a moment looking at herself with bewildered wonder.

She came over.

"You look beautiful," he said. Carly tried to stand up on his stomach, lost her balance and dived for the floor. Becoming something of an expert, he caught her and set her safely on her behind.

"Three points touching," he told the baby. "You'll want to know that when we start climbing mountains together."

"Damon, what on earth do things cost in here?" Rachel whispered. "There's no tags on anything."

"Do you leave price tags on gifts you give?" he asked, smiling as Carly once again assumed her football position—legs astride, fanny in the air, hands on his chest.

"Of course not, but—"

"They're gifts. Can't you just accept them gracefully?" Carly, with a grunt of effort, once again pulled herself to standing. Her feet wobbled on his tummy. Her arms began to windmill. Her face got that astonished look on it, and then she fell. He caught her and she gurgled and told him he was a good boy.

He looked back at Rachel, to see she was flouncing away, the salesclerk ready with hands full of more dresses.

"I'm only trying on two more," she announced. "And then I'm choosing one. One," she said, glaring back at him.

He yawned. Carly crawled up onto his chest and yawned, too.

He felt tired and happy. He had stayed awake too long last night pondering the enormity of what he had done. The dressing room door slammed. The salesclerk came by, and smiled indulgently at him, sprawled on the floor.

"Wrap anything that looked good," he instructed her in an undertone, "and that." He pointed at the white negligee. "Wrap that."

"Sir, everything looks good on her. She is astonishing both in her beauty, and the fact that she doesn't entirely recognize it."

He grinned. "I know."

"This is not my place to say this, and I hope you will forgive me if I am out of line, but I knew your late wife very well. I'm Rosalitta."

"She always spoke of you with great regard," Damon said.

"We all miss her very much."

"Thank you," Damon said.

"I wouldn't normally presume to give you advice, but I am getting old, and sometimes I now fancy myself able to see things that youth cannot see. Your beautiful island is in need of a princess, and your heart is in need of a companion. I believe that she—" she nodded toward the closed change room door "—is the one."

Rosalitta was right. She was out of line. But he did forgive her. Because it seemed to him she was only recognizing what he had already recognized. That Rachel was meant to be with him, linked to Roxbury, a woman of unusual power and grace who would grow into herself as the years went by.

"See if you can talk her into trying on a few more things," he said. "Things suitable for a princess."

He was rewarded with one of the most radiant smiles he had ever seen.

Chapter Five

Rachel emerged from the dressing room in her plain jumper again. She felt like Cinderella after the ball. The denim didn't feel nearly as nice swishing against her skin as silk had. And, of course, she didn't look or feel anything like a princess now.

She stopped.

Damon was fast asleep on the floor, her daughter sprawled across his chest, also fast asleep. She studied him, the long sweep of his lashes, the cut of his strong jaw, the line of his cheekbone.

She thought again of his confidence. She suspected that his position in life had required that he be very straitlaced in most areas, but in those precious instances where it was not required of him he was simply able to relax. He did not seem to give a thought to juggling water glasses, or making himself completely at home on a shop floor. Who was going to tell a prince no?

Certainly not the woman who was coming toward her

now, smiling with soft indulgence at the sleeping prince and the baby.

"Oh," she said in a whisper when she saw Rachel was back in her street clothes, "we were just starting to have fun."

Rachel looked at the stack of items in the woman's arms, and glanced back at her sleeping baby and Damon. She shivered at the thought that soon he would be her husband.

"Please," the clerk said, "just a few more. Just for fun. He doesn't look like he's planning on going anywhere for a while."

Rachel looked at him again, and sighed. "Oh, all right."

She took the items the woman handed to her.

"And you have to come out and show me."

"All right," she agreed.

Darn, if it wasn't fun. This time she had been brought two bathing suits, which she tried on, one so naughty she wasn't showing it to anyone. The other was beautiful, a one-piece maillot in black and red with a beautiful knee-length silk sarong. Was her life really going to include hanging around at a swimming pool or beach now? That was so far removed from her life in the past that she had to laugh out loud. She had always been the one looking wistfully out at the nice day before turning back to her computer, trying to think of a comprehensible way to write about office procedures or technical equipment.

Her father had wanted her to teach, and she had started taking the courses without even asking herself what *she* wanted, what her heart yearned for. She had found herself pregnant before she was anywhere near done, but she knew she had excellent writing skills. A technical writing program had allowed her to work in that area, and usually out of her home. Once Carly had come, she tinkered with writing down the bedtime stories that Carly listened to so raptly, even when she was pre-language. Carly's favorite character, and her own, was Miss Widget the Messy, but so far none of the publishers she had offered the story to had shared mother and child's enthusiasm.

Still, she'd always been the one going to work on the summer day, wishing she was the one going to the beach. And inevitably, it had always rained on her days off and holidays!

Now she looked at the bathing suit and what it represented, and laid it carefully on top of the green silk skirt set she had also decided to keep.

She tried on walking shorts and blouses and slacks and skirts, and modeled them all for the enthusiastic woman, who eventually introduced herself as Rosalitta, the owner of the wonderful boutique. Damon snoozed on, his lips now faintly parted, Carly drooling a pool onto his beautiful sweater.

Rachel had never owned clothes of this quality and marveled at how they looked—how the expense of them made them fit so differently than clothes she had worn before.

"I'm taking these two only," she finally said to Rosalitta, who demurred with a quick "Yes, ma'am." Rachel tried to think if she had ever been called ma'am before. Was it a sign of aging, or had coming in on the arm of the right man earned her such respect?

A thought assailed her. Was there something wrong with getting her respect from who she was with, rather than from who she was?

She was chewing this over, trying to smooth her hair back in place, when Rosalitta knocked on the door.

"Just one more," the woman pleaded. "Try this one.

I just saw it come into the store a few minutes ago, and I have never seen a dress so suited to a person. Please just try it on.''

Rachel glanced out over her shoulder. Damon's chest was still rising and falling, and Carly was still happily ensconced there, so she took the hanger from the woman and closed the door.

The dress she looked at was simply unbelievable. It was an ivory-colored silk, a beautifully beaded matching shawl tossed over one shoulder. Rachel removed the shawl and hung it up, then looked at the dress more carefully.

It was exquisite, a dress that a woman with far more sophistication than she possessed would wear. It had narrow spaghetti straps at the shoulders, a delicately scooped neckline, and then fell in a straight, graceful line. She could not look at the dress without wondering what it would look like on her, and so one last time, she took off her clothes. She deliberately kept her back to the mirror and then slowly turned when she had adjusted the dress.

She gasped.

She truly had become Cinderella.

Gone was the harried mother, the worried sister, the disappointing daughter. In this dress even the mess her hair had become now looked wild and free, as if she had planned it that way.

Her eyes looked as bottomless as the ocean, and her complexion looked like a ripe peach. The dress clung, and hinted, and then clung again. Rachel retrieved the shawl and draped it over her shoulders.

She sighed. The dress had become demure and virginal, hinting at what was underneath. If she was *really* marrying Damon, she thought, this would be the dress she would choose. It was a dress that would make any woman feel like a queen, feel as though a glass slipper had been placed on her foot. For a while.

Until now, Rachel had deliberately ignored the jewelry that had been brought in to accessorize the various outfits, but now she looked through it, and found a simple gold chain, a slender gold bracelet and a pair of tiny gold dew-drop earrings.

The result was spectacular, and she could not take the dress off without sharing it with her enthusiastic cheering section of one, Rosalitta. Sliding her feet into the shoes that had been provided, she stepped carefully out the door.

Rosalitta was nowhere to be seen.

She tiptoed over to Damon and looked again at the sleeping face of her prince.

That was backward, she thought. Just a little backward. It was supposed to be the *princess* who slept.

She found herself dropping to her knees beside him.

He would never know. And now that she had asked him not to kiss her, she might never taste his lips again.

Just this one last time, when she looked so much like a princess, she would allow herself this.

She held back her hair, so that it would not brush his cheek and wake him, and then she lowered her head to his. She touched his cheek with her lips, and marveled at the coarseness beginning to sprout there. When he did not move, she closed her eyes and touched her lips with his. Gently, so as not to awaken him.

His lips looked so firm and yet were so soft. If they had a taste, she would think they tasted like rain. Fresh and clean.

And the kiss did exactly to her what it always did to the princess in fairy tales.

It awoke her.

Something that had long slumbered within her shook

itself awake, and unfolded. It was the woman in her, a full-grown woman with desires and needs, awakening, and she knew it and felt its power with such reality that she reared back from it, and sprang to her feet.

She could feel diamonds of tears gathering in her eyes. She looked up to see Rosalitta standing on the stair leading to the change rooms, frozen.

"I'm sorry," the woman murmured, "I didn't mean to intrude. I shouldn't have watched, but you look so beautiful in that dress. Like something out of a dream. No, a fairy tale."

Carly chose that moment to wake with an indignant squawk that quickly became a wail.

Damon's eyes shot open, brown shot through with gold. He reached for Carly as if by instinct, but his eyes were locked on Rachel, astounded.

"My God," he growled, "you are beautiful."

With one more look at her daughter who was now howling, Rachel turned on her heel and ran into the dressing room. Her shoe fell off, and she left it, opting instead for the sanctuary of the change room. She closed the door, leaned on it, her breast rising and falling as though she had just run a thousand miles.

And really she had. A thousand miles through some unknown part of her very own heart.

Quickly she shed the dress and tugged on her jumper and her blouse. Carly's howling had now softened to little insulted hiccups.

Taking a deep breath, raking a hand through hair which now refused to be tamed and leaped around her face in static waves, she put her chin up and marched out the door.

Damon was trying desperately to make Carly smile. Carly had fixed him with her most intimidating scowl, and sobbed and hiccupped in between listening to the funny voices he was making.

"I think it's been a long day for her," Rachel said, plucking her baby off his knee. "We should go home." She knew she was trying to backtrack over some of that thousand miles, but when she looked into his eyes, she knew the territory she had lost was gone forever. There would be no going back from the wild yearnings his lips had introduced to her heart.

"Were we going to look at a ring?" he asked. "And a few items for Carly?"

"I don't want a ring," she said. "It would be like telling the whole world something we're not ready to tell them."

Damon dropped Rachel and the baby off a little while later. He wondered what whim had made him pick up the shoe that had come off Rachel's foot and put it in his pocket. As if it were a glass slipper. Well, he was already one up on Prince Charming, because he knew exactly who the shoe belonged to.

Damon had arranged to have *everything* that Rachel tried on delivered to Roxbury with the exception of the one dress. A magical dress, because when she had kissed him in it, and he had pretended to still sleep while her lips touched his, feather-soft, he had felt for the first time like a prince. Oh, he had always *known* he was a prince, and accepted that, but it was the first time he had felt as if he owned the whole earth, as if the very stars would order themselves to his command.

The dress was boxed and waiting on his hotel bed for him when he got in, and he wrote a quick note and stuck it among the folds and tissue paper.

He wished he had arranged to take her out for dinner,

but when they left the store he had felt how skittish she was, and he knew he had to be patient, take his time, just like with the young horses he rode. If you tried to force yourself on them, they wanted only to run away. Though he had known Rachel only a short time, he could not bear the idea of her running away.

A soft tap sounded on his door, and Phillip came in, looking very somber, despite the fact his arms were full of boxes and bags from various children's stores. "I just got word on that flight I checked for you. Victoria Rockford was on it."

Damon let nothing show in his face, because he had not even shared with Phillip, his most trusted employee, who Victoria really was. But inside he felt a twist of anxiety. Rachel's intuitions were correct. And he suspected his own were, too. That Rachel's sister was the illegitimate daughter of Victor Thorton. Victoria Rockford was the heir who had been kidnapped, he was growing more and more certain of that.

While Phillip waited, Damon scribbled a hasty note and sealed it in an envelope. "I want you to deliver this to Roland Thorton. Tonight. Within the hour if you can. He's returned here to Thortonburg. It's urgent."

Damon now knew he had to marry Rachel as soon as possible. He wanted to provide shelter when the storm hit, and he felt it was going to hit very, very soon.

He waited a few moments, collecting himself, and then he picked up the phone. The first call he made was the important one. He called Brother Raymond.

Briefly he explained his circumstances, and what he needed done.

Brother Raymond did not condemn him, but his voice was laced with caution. "You are rushing things. How will you ever know if anyone will ever love you for the man you are, instead of the fact you are a prince, and can provide for them?''

Damon was not at all happy with his friend for introducing this element of doubt to his plans.

"It's not about me," he said fiercely, "it's about her. She needs me, now."

"Bah. You need *her* now. You are a man dying of loneliness and too proud to admit it."

"Will you perform the ceremony, or should I ask someone else?"

The good brother sighed. "Damon, you know I will do anything for you. Besides, I would not miss an opportunity to see for myself what is *really* going on."

"Nothing is *really* going on. It is exactly as I told you."

"Then why are you so defensive?"

He hung up from Brother Damon, feeling at odds with himself. He looked at the long list of business calls he had to return as a result of his family's shipping interests. The Montagues had not only been awarded the Royal Wynborough shipping contract, but they had also been given deed and title to Thorton Shipping, a gesture that, along with Roland and Lily's romance, had gone a long way toward defusing the feud between the two royal families.

He raked a hand through his hair. What was he going to tell Rachel? He could not withhold the information about her sister being on the plane. He slipped the box with the dress in it under his arm and went to see Rachel.

As soon as she saw him, she knew. "What have you found out about Victoria?"

"I don't want you to panic. But she was on that flight back."

Rachel began to cry, and he gathered her in his arms. "Tomorrow morning," he said, "we're going to talk to your father. And tomorrow afternoon we're going to Roxbury and getting married.''

She nodded against him, and he felt overwhelmed by her trust. He suspected she was an independent woman, fiercely so, but she was trusting him with her sister's life—and her own. He thought of Brother Raymond's doubts, and hoped he was worthy of her trust.

She wore the ivory dress. He wore a beautifully tailored charcoal suit, and white silk shirt. She clutched the lovely bouquet of spring flowers with sweating hands.

They were in a little stone church, perched on the edge of a rocky cliff that overlooked a tossing sea.

Rachel had never been to Roxbury before, and if she had not been so nervous, she thought her breath would have been taken away by the verdant loveliness of the pastures with their fat contented cattle, the woods with their noisy birds, the peaceful small lakes and ponds they passed, and the miles of uninhabited seaside and beaches.

Today had passed in a whirl, starting with a very disturbing visit with her father, who seemed more delighted that a prince was in his house than perturbed that his daughter was missing. When they confronted him with the fact that she had been on the airplane, he said he knew she was back on the island, but she had told him she was going to visit a friend on her return. But when Rachel pressed him about what friend and confronted him that he'd told Heidi that Victoria had been delayed on the continent, he became vague and slightly hostile. Damon had ended the interview abruptly, but with courtesy, obviously not wanting her father to become aware of their suspicion that he was somehow involved in her sister's disappearance.

They had come to Roxbury by helicopter, a trip that

delighted Carly and nauseated Rachel. Then Carly had been left at the castle, in the charge of a cheerful teenage girl named Bonnie, who was the cook's daughter. When Rachel left them, they had been building blocks together on the kitchen floor under the indulgent eye of the cook.

Rachel did not want to think about that castle. It looked exactly like all the castles in storybooks, with its stone walls and soaring turrets. Inside the furnishings were rich and formal. She had looked around the few rooms she had seen and had the sinking sensation, *I will never feel at home here.*

Damon had left her in the care of a lovely young house-maid, who had showed her where to change into her dress.

"Where does Damon live?" she had asked, looking around the room with its high ceilings, ghastly portraits and French Provincial furniture with mounting horror.

"He has his own apartments, miss. They're a bit cozier than this."

And then a chauffeur had whisked her off to this little chapel, and Damon had been waiting for her.

Now she stood in this pretty little church, trembling, the light pouring through stained glass windows making everything seem as though it couldn't possibly be real.

Brother Raymond looked to her just like Friar Tuck in his brown hooded robe, knotted at the waist with a piece of white cotton rope. He had spoken to her before the ceremony, and asked her quietly and gently if she knew her heart. If she was sure of what she was doing. He had looked vaguely troubled.

The strength of her response had surprised her.

But Damon seemed to her to be a stranger, remote and frightening. Had she really expected tenderness as he said those age-old words?

Damon was sliding the ring on her finger and looking

down at her with a look she could not decipher. Haunted might have described it. Which was not how any bride wanted her groom to look, even a bride who was aware that their arrangement was strictly business.

And now it was her turn, and she was repeating the words after Brother Raymond, and she heard her voice wobbling with a doubt she had not had before this moment, before seeing the look on Damon's face as he passed deeper and deeper into territory from which there was no return.

"You may kiss the bride."

The words took her by surprise, though, of course, they should not have.

Damon looked askance at her, and she knew they had to make an exception to their rule this once.

She leaned toward him, and found herself rising on her toes to meet his lips.

They touched, and lingered. It should have been a quick kiss, sealing the deal, but it was not quick at all. And she did not break it off.

When the old friar finally cleared his throat, they both snapped apart and turned to face him. Rachel could feel the wild blush in her cheeks. She stole a look at Damon. He had lost some of the impassive look that had carried him through the ceremony, but not enough that she felt reassured. She could not help but notice that Brother Raymond had finally lost that vaguely troubled look and was beaming at them both.

He blessed them and they turned away from him. It was only then she became aware of two people, obviously trusted servants, standing in the shadows, witnesses to the marriage.

They left the church into the bright sunshine. Rachel noticed the daffodils blooming in the gardens around the church, and took a deep breath. Damon seemed stiff and uneasy beside her, the first time since she had known him that he did not seem one hundred percent sure of himself.

"What is it?" she asked him. "Damon?"

Damon tried to compose his features so she would not sense his deep distress. It was not until he had stood before Brother Raymond and the ceremony had begun that he became aware of a feeling inside of himself that he had only felt on one or two other occasions in his life.

It was a feeling of doing something deeply wrong, against his soul. A feeling of betraying his own sense of integrity.

When he looked at her, though, he still felt that marrying her was right.

And then the part that was wrong struck him.

It was a sham. He was not really marrying her. He was *pretending* to marry her. It didn't matter what he said his reasons were, the truth was now staring him in the face.

He was lying.

And worst of all, he was lying before God.

He helped her into his Jaguar—and saw he was not successfully hiding the fact that he now knew he had done something deeply wrong.

He took a deep breath, aware he was entangling himself further by now trying to hide from his wife how he really felt.

"I had a little lunch packed," he told her. "We'll have a small picnic before we go back. Is that all right with you? You're not worried about Carly?"

"Not yet," she said.

"We could go get her."

"No. I'd rather it was just you and me." And then she blushed like the new bride she was. And wasn't. He cursed himself again.

He drove them to a small grove of trees along the same shoreline as the church. As he drove, he told her boyhood stories of his adventures in the various places they passed. A red-eyed slobbering bull had put him up that tree when he was just a lad. There was the place he had got a fish-hook stuck in the most embarrassing of places. He was trying desperately to relieve the anxious expression on her face that he knew he was responsible for.

He finally stopped the car, then came around to help her out before retrieving a big wicker basket from the trunk.

In moments he had spread out a beautiful linen table-cloth on the green, green grass, and was removing strawberries and champagne and French bread and chilled salmon from the basket.

Rachel settled on the blanket, and he was glad to see she intended to own that dress, not let it own her. It seemed to him the dress had been made for this day, and this moment. *If it had been real.*

She poured the champagne, and offered a toast.

"To the future," she said.

"To the future," he agreed. He felt she was easily the most sensuous woman he had ever seen. And now her future held celibacy. Instead of a new groom, he saw himself for what he was. And he was appalled.

He was a thief, who had stolen this beautiful woman's future.

Damon took a different route back to the castle, a winding road that went across the top of the island. He was still not himself, a fact that all his amusing stories could not hide. Rachel sensed a tension between them that had not been there before they had said those irrevocable words, "I do."

So when she saw the little stone cottage at the end of a winding road in a grove of towering trees, she asked him to stop. Because she could bear the tension no more, or because the cottage was so in keeping with the cottage of her dreams, she could not be sure.

"What is it?" he asked.

She nodded in the direction of the house. "That place reminds me of something."

"Of what?" he prodded.

And even though she did not feel as comfortable with him as she had felt yesterday, she found herself telling him, "A dream I once had for Carly and me. To have a little cottage in the country."

"Would you like to go look at it?"

"Oh, no, of course not. It doesn't matter."

But he didn't listen, and he steered the car off the main road and onto the track.

"Damon, what if somebody lives there?"

He laughed. "That house used to belong to one of my cousins. I think it's a relic from the days when we were all little more than pirates plying the high seas. It's been empty for a number of years, I think. It's pretty remote up here."

He stopped the car, and she got out. The cottage made her want to hug herself, it was so lovely. It was indeed empty, and she walked around it, very aware of where she would put the swings and the slide and a little covered sandbox, and window boxes tumbling over with flowers.

"Do you want to go in?"

"It won't be unlocked, will it?"

He laughed. "You obviously have mistaken Roxbury for a much more exciting place than it is. We don't have much in the way of crime here. I think it's probably unlocked."

It was good to hear him laugh, to see a lightening of that grim expression that had been on his face since they had stood side by side in the church. She went up the flagstone steps and touched the door handle—a gold door handle on a white door with a window in it.

The door fell open as if the cottage had been waiting for her.

The floors were stone and wood, the walls thick and cream-colored, the windows with their tiny panes sunk deep into the walls. It was larger than it first seemed with a living room and a dining room, a huge kitchen, and three substantial bedrooms.

The cottage looked empty and somewhat forlorn with dust motes dancing across the floors, and the windows needing a thorough cleaning. Still, she could see exactly what it could—and should—be, and imagined where she would put the furniture, the kind of drapes she would hang, how it would look filled with sunshine and flowers, and how it would feel filled with laughter.

Finally, reluctantly, she turned back to him, smiling. "What a lovely old place. I'm ready to go now." But even as she said the words, she felt dread at returning to the castle.

"It's yours," he said as he closed the door behind them.

"What?" She whirled on him.

"I give it to you. A wedding gift."

"You already gave me the dress."

He laughed. "So I did. I just thought it might be easier for us to live here than at the castle."

She thought of that huge and brooding castle that seemed so silent and formal, with servants hustling here and there, and she felt as if he had given her the sun.

"I would like to live here better."

"Then it's done."

"Damon, don't spoil me."

"I think that would be impossible."

Both of them started in surprise when Phillip knocked and came in the door. "I've been looking all over for you, sir. I saw your car out on the road. I had trouble getting your message through last night, spent a most unpleasant few hours with royal security at the Thorton palace. But I finally did meet with Roland Thorton, and personally gave him your note. Prince Roland has asked me to give you this."

Damon ripped open the envelope that was passed to him, read it, then read it again before he shoved it in his pocket.

"I was asked to tell you he wants you and Miss Rockford to meet with a Mr. Lance Grayson, head of the Investigative Division of the Royal Security Detail, at your earliest convenience."

"It's not Miss Rockford anymore, though for the time, Phillip, I'd like you to keep this to yourself. May I present to you my bride?"

Phillip's face, always completely unflappable, registered shock and then delight.

"I congratulate both of you." He moved forward, took her hand and lifted it to his lips. "Princess."

"Please arrange for the helicopter to run us back to Thortonburg within the hour."

"Damon?" Rachel asked. "What is going on? Why would one of the Thortonburg princes be sending you a message? Why would the head of their Royal Security Detail want to meet *us*?"

Phillip went quietly out the door. And Damon took a deep breath.

"I need to tell you something about your sister."

Chapter Six

She was shaking, partly from the shock of being called "princess" for the first time, and partly because of the grave look on Damon's face.

He led her from the house, back into the bright sunshine. Underneath a massive oak stood a wooden glider swing and he guided her toward it. It faced a phenomenal view—Roxbury castle far below them and to the east, surrounded by lush meadows and woodlands, and beyond that the restless sea. At any other time, it seemed to her, this landscape would call her and soothe her and hold her. Even now, despite her distress, she had an odd feeling of homecoming.

Damon brushed off the seat for her and she wondered if she would ever become accustomed to the natural way in which he treated her like a queen. He settled her on the swing before he sat down beside her.

Again she noted that Damon had not seemed himself since the wedding, and now he looked more troubled than ever.

She made herself focus, forced herself to ignore the scent of him that enveloped her, headier than the scents of the spring day, headier than wine.

"Tell me," she implored him.

He was silent for a moment, and Rachel could tell he was organizing his thoughts, which only filled her with more dread. And then he took her hand in his own.

This, too, seemed right, as if when her strength was at its lowest ebb, he would lend her some of his. And that someday his would be a low ebb, and she would give him hers. She felt this was a vow between them, even though it remained unspoken.

"Roland Thorton told me that at the coronation celebration of King Phillip of Wynborough a note had surfaced. Kept top secret, it claimed that the grand duke's illegitimate daughter had been kidnapped."

Rachel recalled, vaguely, a media feeding frenzy around the coronation anniversary event just a short while ago. It had seemed so unrelated to her plain and ordinary life that she had largely ignored it. Station, she could ignore. Pain, she could not.

"My God, what a harrowing thing. I can imagine the terror I would feel if something like that happened to Carly," Rachel said, and understood that seeming to have everything in the world was not all it appeared. Perhaps, sometimes, it just made a person a desirable target. "That poor, poor child, an innocent victim in all this."

"She's not exactly a child. The duke's daughter is full grown."

"It's not common knowledge, is it, that the duke had a daughter? Something else I've missed by not being a great reader of the tabs."

Why did his eyes look so sympathetic?

"No, it's not common knowledge. Even the tabs never

dug that out. But someone did, and they have used the knowledge in the most terrible way. Because of the bad blood between our two families, Roland took it upon himself to come to Roxbury to see if *we* were the perpetrators of this crime.''

''That's absurd. You? He doesn't know you at all, does he?'' She was a little shocked at how defensive she felt of the man who had been her husband for less than an hour, and a part of her life for less than a week.

''Well, he certainly sees the Montagues in a brand-new light, all right,'' Damon said with a hint of dryness.

''Damon, this is fascinating and horrible, but I can't for the life of me see what it has to do with Victoria.''

''Can't you?'' he asked, watching her closely.

''No!''

''Does it strike you as odd that two young ladies would go missing at the same time?''

''Are you saying you think there might be a serial killer about, or a serial kidnapper?'' At the very thought her heart lurched inside her chest, and began to pound painfully. ''But nobody in my family has received a ransom note!''

''I guess I was hoping there was an easy way to say what needs to be said, and there is not.''

''Please just say it.''

''Rachel, Victoria is Victor Thorton's illegitimate daughter.''

She felt her mouth drop open, and she pulled her hand from his, feeling betrayed by him. ''No, she isn't. That's utterly impossible. Ridiculous.'' She scanned his face to see if his eyes were laughing. He was a man who juggled in posh restaurants, after all. Maybe he didn't know what was funny and what wasn't. A reminder that he really was a stranger to her, no matter how good his hand felt in hers.

"Why would you say such a thing to me? My sister is my sister."

"Rachel—"

"She's not anyone's illegitimate daughter."

But even as she said it, looking into the pain in his face, she knew he would not be telling her this if he did not believe it absolutely to be true. And it penetrated her dismay that if it were true, for the first time she would understand Malcolm's inexplicable bitterness toward Victoria. Even so, everything in her rebelled against it.

"Can you prove it?" she asked stiffly.

He looked away from her, ran a hand through his hair, and then looked back at her. He took a deep breath.

"Was your mother's name Maribelle?"

Rachel nodded, feeling as if a weight was descending on her. "Yes," she whispered.

"Was her maiden name Leighton?" he asked gently.

"Oh, God."

He took a deep breath. "Does your sister have an unusual raspberry birthmark on her left hip? In the shape of a teardrop?"

"How could you know that?" she asked, and when he was silent, she finally said it out loud, "How could you know that, unless it was true?"

He took the letter from his pocket. "Last night I had Phillip deliver an urgent letter to Roland Thorton, outlining the details of your sister's disappearance as I knew them. This is his answer. The Grand Duke of Thortonburg confirms he had an affair with Maribelle Leighton nearly twenty-eight years ago."

The math, Rachel realized, was not difficult. Her sister was twenty-seven.

"He had no idea the liaison produced a child. Until now. The birthmark was mentioned in the ransom note. Unknown to the public, that mark is hereditary to the Thortons."

Rachel could not look into the deep sympathy in his eyes any longer. She looked, instead, to the tossing waters of the far-off sea. She wanted for it not to be true, for so many reasons. Because it changed reality as she had always perceived it. Because it meant her shadowy feeling that something bad had happened to Victoria had just become something very concrete, frighteningly real. Her sister, her beloved sister, was in danger.

"If Victoria isn't Malcolm's," she thought out loud, "why the ruse? Why didn't they just tell us? A one-line statement would have sufficed. 'Girls, you don't have the same father.'"

She realized that she was babbling and that Damon could not answer her questions, anyway. And she knew her father, though a young man in the Sixties, had never indulged in the free love philosophies of that age.

She pushed these questions aside, only to have them replaced with fear. The fear was spearlike in its intensity. She tried to think where Victoria might be, what she might be going through. Was she tied up? Terrified? Or fighting mad?

"My sister has been kidnapped," she said dully, as if saying it would make it somehow more real, and it did. She looked back at him. His face was swimming in front of her eyes, the gold in them like beacons she had to try and swim toward. "Oh, my God, Damon, what am I going to do? My sister is in danger. I have to—"

He took both her hands in his, and squeezed hard. "Listen to me, Rachel. Listen. You have to keep calm. Do you understand? You have to keep your head."

She took a deep breath. And then another. She felt the strength of his hands on hers, felt the calm in his eyes. And then she whispered, "I'm so afraid."

He pulled her close to him, and she wept into his shirt.

"I don't know who I have ever cried on more," she said finally.

"I don't know of anyone who ever deserved a shoulder to cry on more."

"What am I going to do?"

"Everything you can. We'll meet with Lance Grayson as soon as it can be arranged. We may have information that will be helpful to him, and he may have some that will be reassuring to us."

"Us? She's *my* sister. You haven't even met her. Why do you care so much?"

He smiled. "She's my sister-in-law. She's part of you."

"Why do you care so much about me?"

"I don't know, Rachel."

"You're irresistibly attracted to lost puppies."

She wanted him to deny it, but he didn't.

Instead he said, "Brother Raymond gave me a little prayer to say after my wife and son died. It has helped me immeasurably, though I have never considered myself a man of religion."

"Will you tell it to me?"

"God, grant me the serenity to accept the things I cannot change,
The courage to change the things I can,
And the wisdom to know the difference."

"The Serenity Prayer," Rachel said, and then repeated the prayer in her mind, and found it did have power. She could not change the fact that her sister had been kidnapped, all she could change was her own reaction to it. And she had to find within herself the calm that would allow her to be helpful in any way she could be.

"Damon," she told him with a weak smile, "this could well go down in history as the world's worst honeymoon."

"The honeymoon wasn't going to be spent in, er, quite the traditional manner anyway."

She blushed when she caught his meaning.

"We need to go back to Thortonburg right away," he said. "Will you feel all right leaving Carly here while we go?"

Rachel thought of trying to deal with Carly's needs and demands, and knew it would be harder to focus on what needed to be done to find her sister.

"If you want to bring her, I can arrange to have her looked after."

"Mind reader," she said. "I want to leave her here. This place, this island, feels safe, Damon. And suddenly all the world feels unsafe and scary."

"I'll never let anything happen to Carly."

"Thank you."

"Or to you."

His voice was fierce and firm, and these vows she knew meant as much to him as his wedding vows had. Maybe more, since they did not create the same unsettled look in the depths of his eyes.

She took a breath, and then laughed shakily. "Would you like to hear something ironic?"

"What?"

"My sister and I both seem to have become princesses this week."

They drove back to the castle, and this time Damon did

not pull up at the main entrance, but rather at an entrance to one of the wings.

These were his apartments, and Rachel could not find much about them that was cozy. Though the rooms were smaller than those in the part of the castle she had seen, she still found them formal and intimidating with their high ceilings and thick carpets and heavy brocaded draperies. He took her down a long hallway with gloomy pictures of his ancestors.

"I know," he said when he glanced at her and saw her looking at them, "they're a grim-looking bunch."

"Not a juggler among them," she acknowledged.

He opened double doors at the end of the hall, and they were in a master suite. A huge bed dominated the room. French doors went out onto a private terrace. Another door went through to an en suite, and a door off that led to a smaller bedroom.

Rachel thought this smaller bedroom to be the nicest room she had seen in the house—bright and friendly.

"This is perfect," she breathed, and saw how really perfect it was. No one would ever know after they went through those double doors at night, where they slept. It was a perfect arrangement for two people pretending to be married.

Pretending. She hadn't thought of it quite like that before, and now she found it disturbing.

Was it not possible they would form a strong partnership, a marriage, in every sense of the word, except one?

Somehow, being this close to the intimacy of his bedroom, she was no longer so certain about that.

Damon reminded her they had urgent business to get to.

She noticed the boxes from the dress shop neatly

stacked against one wall of the smaller bedroom. She wanted to protest his generosity, but didn't have it in her.

She was a princess now, and she needed to look the part. He had understood that from the beginning, and inwardly she was thankful to him for once again looking after her.

He went out the door and closed it behind him. In a moment she heard the shower running, and felt her face grow hot at the idea of living in such close proximity to him.

How was she going to keep her hands off of him?

She reminded herself, sternly, that she had much bigger concerns at the moment. She tore into the boxes, and threw on the first suitable outfit she could find, a beige pantsuit.

The shower had turned off, and awkwardly she went through the room still clouded with steam. She stopped for a minute, letting the steam that had touched him touch her.

She realized this marriage had put her in grave danger of becoming pathetic.

She tapped lightly on his door.

"Come in."

She entered the room, and stopped. He was in trousers, but naked from the waist up. He was toweling his hair dry and it curled around his neck and ears.

His body was magnificent, muscular and lean, his skin satiny and gold, a whorl of dark hair matted on his exquisite chest, arrowing down to the slender hard muscles of his lean stomach.

Her mouth went dry. This marriage had put her in *very* grave danger of becoming pathetic.

"Is this the only way out of here?" she asked, her eyes trying to go everywhere but to him, but always finding their way back. "I want to give Carly a quick kiss and cuddle before we go."

If he noticed her awkwardness, it didn't show. He, typically, had no self-consciousness at all. "It is the only door. We can put another in, if you want. Or trade bedrooms. Or move to Cliff Croft."

She registered the name of the cottage they had looked at with delight.

"I'm sure we'll figure it out," she said. "Which way is Carly?"

"If you'll wait, I'll come with you. I don't think you'll find it on your own, and besides I'd like to see her, too."

She watched as he put on his shirt, feeling more and more desperate. It was as if she had sentenced herself to life. He was gorgeous. He made the blood sing through her veins. And she had agreed to a marriage in name only.

A mistake.

The time to back out was now. Right now.

And yet even now part of her was willing to accept what he offered. To not be with him at all would surely be worse than to be with him and not touch him.

Marginally.

He led her through the labyrinth that was his home. They found Carly still in the kitchen. Somehow Rachel had imagined her daughter would be waiting anxiously for her, but Carly was standing on a chair at the table with Bonnie hovering. She was cutting out cookies with a cookie cutter, and sampling the dough at the same time.

She gave her mother a quick glance, and then, tongue caught between her only teeth, she pressed down the soft plastic cutter. And smiled.

Rachel went over to see Carly's work. She had made a Christmas tree, and Bonnie picked it up and put it on a cookie tray beside a Santa and a reindeer.

"We only had Christmas cookie cutters," she apologized shyly.

Obviously Carly couldn't have cared less. She was covered in flour and dough, and she looked gloriously happy.

"Mommy has to go out for a while," Rachel said.

"Kay, bye," Carly said, already busy selecting her next cutter from a large bowl of them at her side.

Rachel kissed Carly. Damon snitched a ball of dough, put it in his mouth, and kissed Carly on the cheek. Carly threw her doughy hands around him, leaving flour marks on his fresh shirt.

He was still brushing at them when the car was brought around for them at the front door. He smiled at Rachel. "I kind of like being a daddy," he told her softly.

If it were not for her missing sister, and the fact she and Damon were not going to be making babies together, she thought her life would be just about perfect.

She seemed to be sitting very stiffly next to him as he pulled the car up to the helicopter pad. He supposed she was consumed with worry about her sister, and he had recognized she disliked flying on their way to Roxbury earlier.

He let his mind drift back to that moment when she had come into his bedroom.

It was then it had been confirmed in his own mind the exact proportions of his mistake.

He'd seen the way her eyes rested on his naked skin, and then skittered away, and then came back again.

Everything in him had longed to go to her, to place her hands on the heat of his skin, to take her lips with his.

But he was the one who had made this foolish bargain.

What had he been thinking? That he was made of steel, rather than flesh? He'd been thinking of nothing but her lips ever since Brother Raymond had told him he could kiss her.

What had he done? He'd married her, and told her it was strictly business. And now he had to be a man of honor.

If she wanted something else, he would have to allow her the first move.

One thing that amazed him was how the grief had dried up inside him. It was not that he had dismissed Sharon and Samuel, but rather that he recognized they were a part of who he had become, they would always go on inside of him, but that he was ready to live again, too.

Why hadn't he recognized that sooner? He could have proposed a real marriage.

She would have said no to a real marriage. They barely knew each other.

At least, he amended, on the physical plane. On that other plane, the one of mystery and unknown, he thought perhaps they had known each other for a very long time indeed.

He wanted to take her hand. But he didn't. And he wished, for all the world, he could seize back those vulnerable words he had said about being a daddy.

The Thorton palace was even more intimidating than the Montague one. Damon and Rachel were ushered into a plush office furnished in a distinctively masculine way.

Lance Grayson was waiting for them.

Rachel's first impression of him was that he was a man who possessed both fierce strength and icy composure. This impression was underscored when he took her hand in his firm grasp. Though he was a stranger to her, she felt the raw confidence in him. She felt that if anyone was capable of finding Victoria, it would be this formidable man.

A bond formed almost instantly between Grayson and Damon—two strong men recognizing each other.

After the introductions, they all took chairs in a semi-circle, facing one another.

Grayson leaned toward her, elbows on knees, powerful hands knit together. "I'm very sorry," he began quietly, "that your sister and the grand duke's daughter are one and the same person. I understand this has probably come as a shock to you."

"It has." She saw Lance give a quick look to Damon.

"I don't want to add any further grief, Miss Rockford, I'm sure you know that, but your sister's safety is paramount to all of us."

"More grief?"

"I have reason to believe your father may be behind your sister's disappearance."

In a way, having her own worst fears confirmed was a nightmare. And yet there was the finest little thread of relief running through her horror. Her intuition had told her her father was involved, and it had been correct. For some reason, knowing she could trust her intuition was very important to her right now. For was it not intuition that had told her it would be all right to say yes to Damon's bizarre proposal that they marry each other?

"I have wondered, ever since Victoria went missing, what my father's involvement might be," she admitted unsteadily, and felt Damon's hand creep around hers and squeeze it.

"Have you?" Grayson asked with intent interest. "Tell me why."

She told him her reasons. It actually felt good to be taken seriously.

He looked at her thoughtfully. "I think you are a very intelligent and levelheaded young woman, Miss Rockford. Have you told anyone else this?"

"I reported my sister missing to the police. A friend of my father's at the police station took the report, so naturally I didn't mention anything about suspecting my own father. I was made to feel silly enough that I was reporting her missing."

"Who was the friend?"

"Sergeant Lloyd Crenshaw."

Grayson jotted down the name. "Anyone else?"

"I told Damon. Oh, and Victoria's friend, Heidi Ramsey, knows I'm looking for my sister."

"All right. And that's all?" When she nodded, he continued, "I'm conducting this investigation in secret with the cooperation of Lieutenant Jacks with the Thortonburg police. If she wants to speak to you, feel free to tell her what you have told me, but no one else."

"I understand."

"Miss Rockford, I am going to ask you something else. As you think more and more about the possibility of your father being involved, you are quite naturally going to feel more and more angry. I don't want you to confront your father, or even hint at what you suspect to him, or to anyone else."

"I understand."

He was watching her closely. "Your sister's life could be placed in very grave danger if you did."

She wanted to leap to her father's defense, to say he would never actually hurt Victoria, but, of course, in light of what it seemed he might have done, to say that would be ridiculous.

"I think more of this investigation hinges on you than you realize," Grayson told her quietly.

"In what way?"

"If your father is responsible, it's possible that somewhere in you is the memory that will unlock Victoria's whereabouts. Can you think of a place he might have taken her?"

Rachel thought. "His life really is very narrow, Mr. Grayson. Aside from the school basement, or the sheds on the grounds, I don't think I can help you."

"I'll check both of those—without alerting him, naturally. I'll send someone to check the basement on excuse of checking the boilers, and an extra 'gardener' can check the grounds and sheds. You've been to his home recently. There were no sounds, nothing out of the ordinary? A sign of a struggle, perhaps?"

"No. Victoria wasn't at the house."

"How do you know that with such certainty?"

"We grew up with a dog, Ginger. It adored Victoria. If she shut her bedroom door, the dog would whine outside until she gave in and opened it. Ginger was quite content at my father's feet the whole time Damon and I were there."

"Good observation. Meanwhile, if you think of anything, even something that seems small and insignificant, I want you to call. I've put your name on my priority list and you'll be put through immediately on my cell or office phone if you call."

To be treated with such respect after her night at the police station was quietly rewarding. And he didn't even know she was a princess. She had a feeling Lance Grayson was the kind of man you had to earn respect from.

"And where can I get in touch with you?" he asked.

She looked at Damon.

"We're going to be in Roxbury. I'll make sure that

your name is also on my priority list so that you can get through to Rachel or myself in an instant if you need to.''

''Both of you are going to be in Roxbury?''

''That's correct.''

''Do you mind me asking why? According to what you've told me here, you only just met at the police station a few nights ago.''

''I'm sure I can trust you to keep a confidence, as well, Mr. Grayson?''

He nodded.

''Rachel and I were married this morning.''

That hard glance went from one to the other. ''No offense, Your Highness, but fairy tales are things you tell your children. Nobody falls in love that quickly.''

Rachel cringed, thinking Damon would say that their relationship had nothing to do with love.

But he didn't. He smiled without rancor, looked at her and said, ''I would have said the same thing myself a few days ago.''

''Well, have a great honeymoon,'' Lance said rather cynically.

''It will be much better once you find my sister,'' Rachel told him, getting to her feet.

The hardness left his eyes.

''Princess, you have my word that I will do everything in my power to find your sister. Everything.''

She studied him for a moment, and his considerable power was evident. She had a feeling when he did find Victoria enough sparks would fly between them to make fireworks.

She believed he would find Victoria if she could be found, and she left, feeling much calmer than when she had arrived.

''Damon, before we go home, could we stop at Mrs.

Brumble's little cottage?'' She realized she had called Roxbury home, and pondered that for a moment. She had tossed together a few items for her journey to Roxbury, and truth be told, had very little in the way of possessions, but now she remembered something she wanted.

When he stopped at her place, she went up the walk and entered. She looked around and already the cottage seemed tiny. She knew she would have to get back soon to do a final clean-up and sort out what she wanted and what she didn't, but Damon had told her to leave it for the time being. He said there would be a more settled period in her life to look after these details.

Meanwhile, she had forgotten something most precious to her. Her photo albums.

She scooped them up in her arms, and brought them out to the car. Perhaps Lance Grayson had been right. There was a clue to her sister's whereabouts buried some-where in her memory and these books might help get it out.

She scooped the mail out of her box on the way. Wedged between a stack of bills was an envelope with the return address of a children's publisher where she had sent her story about Miss Widget the Messy. She knew just by the shape and thinness of the envelope what it was—another rejection—and tried not to feel so forlorn about it.

Today she had begun a new life that had nothing to do with telling silly stories to children.

''Are those bills?'' Damon asked. ''Toss them in the back. Phillip will look after them.''

She tossed them in the back, but not before she warned him she would look after them herself. Then, settling her albums on her lap, she yawned wearily and in a gesture that was unconsciously but completely trusting she put her head on Damon's shoulder and went to sleep.

Chapter Seven

"Can I help you, sir?"

Damon smiled. The woman in his arms was fast asleep, snuggled into him like a trusting child. "If you get the door, that will be fine."

Phillip went up the stairs in front of him, and opened the door.

Damon realized he was carrying Rachel over the threshold, and allowed himself to wish, for just a second, that it was real. That she was awake and looking into his eyes with deep wonder and excitement and anticipation.

"Phillip, could you just grab that mail in the back of the car, and see that her bills are looked after?"

"Of course, sir."

He went up the thickly carpeted stairs, nudged open the door to his bedroom. He couldn't believe how heavily she slept and then he realized that she was exhausted.

It had been too much for her. Getting married. Finding out her sister was not her full sister. And that her sister had been kidnapped.

He thought she had handled these events with uncommon grace and courage, and saw now that they had taken far more of a toll on her than she had let him see.

He hesitated at his bed, wanting to put her in it, feeling she belonged there, but he could hear Brother Raymond accusing him of being the one with the need, and he felt a desire to prove Brother Raymond wrong, even though in his heart he was facing the fact that Brother Raymond had been right.

He saw a crib had been set up in the adjoining bedroom, and the light from his own bedroom caught on the round apples of Carly's cheeks. Carefully, he put Rachel on the bed, removed her shoes, pulled the covers up over her.

She muttered something, and he listened, hoping he would make some sense of it, but that didn't happen.

For a long moment, he gazed down at her. Brother Raymond had been right. How would he ever know now if Rachel could have come to love him for the man he was? Why had he never really had that expectation that someday someone would love him for who he was, instead of what he was?

Rachel cried out suddenly in her sleep. "Victoria!"

He leaned over and touched her. "It's all right, Rachel, I'm here."

This seemed to soothe her, and her hand took his and held it, strong even in sleep. He found himself unwilling to let loose her hand, and so he sat on the edge of the bed. And then, after a while, he thought he would lie down for just a minute.

He would lie down beside her, just as if he had really carried her across the threshold. He would drink in the smell of her just this once.

He should let go of her, he thought wearily, and find his own bed, but it was as if his thoughts found their way into her dreams, because her hand tightened and she moaned restlessly.

He thought of Brother Raymond, and what he had done this day, and suddenly felt tired beyond weariness. Promising himself it was just for a moment, he closed his eyes.

Rachel woke to feel warmth and weight beside her. She sat up, disoriented. "Carly!"

Her eyes adjusted to the room, and she saw it was the small bedroom in Damon's apartments and that Carly was sleeping peacefully in a crib just across the room.

How had she gotten from his car to here?

She had always been a heavy sleeper, but she thought this probably took the cake. She realized that she was still fully dressed, the new outfit crushed. And then she saw that Damon slept beside her, fully dressed, and she felt such tenderness for him. He was such a good man.

She touched his hair, and his eyes opened sleepily and then focused and he smiled.

"What are you doing here?" she whispered.

"You were having a bad dream," he whispered back, and she liked his voice sleep roughened to a growl. It was sexy.

"How did I get here?"

"I carried you."

"Damon, you should have woken me up. You'll have given yourself a bad back."

"Right. You weigh about as much as a feather. You were calling your sister in your dreams."

"I know. I dreamt about her, and then I started having terrible dreams that Carly was missing, too. I'm scared to go back to sleep"

He pulled her close to him. "I'll stay, for as long as you need me."

And suddenly he knew that was true. He had talked her into this marriage, and it had been wrong. Not for him. For her. Wrong to deprive her of all the things her wedding night and falling in love and getting married would have given her.

He had seen it as a solution to his problems, and not looked any further than that, and now he knew only one way to make amends to her.

To keep it the way he had promised it would be. A relationship based on business. And to keep it that way only until he could see clearly that she no longer needed him. He would shelter her through this storm with her sister, make sure she was on her feet, and then he would let her go.

Having just made this decision, he was stunned when she reached up and touched his cheek with soft and gentle hands.

She came to him and offered her lips, and he took them.

She tasted so sweet. Of buttercups and spring afternoons. And innocence.

It occurred to him, despite her life experiences, she was largely innocent.

But it was not innocence that held him captive, but a hint of something just beyond the innocence, a slight parting of her lips, a soft sound that came deep from within her, a sound of hunger and wanting.

Goaded by that soft sound, he covered the silken plumpness of her lips with his mouth more aggressively, allowing a hunger and a wanting he had not known he possessed to telegraph itself to her through a language as old as the earth itself.

He felt her breath quicken, and his arms went around her, one around the sweet feminine curve of her shoulders, the other hand splayed across the small of her back, pressing her into him. He could feel the entire length of her, supple, soft, strong, melt into him, and was not sure if he had ever felt such exquisite torment.

Her breath was becoming ragged, and so was his. He could feel his heartbeat and hers, beating together, a primal drum, the tempo increasing.

He tasted her lips once more, then parted them with his tongue, entered the hollow of her mouth, heard her gasp of delight, felt her shiver of wanting, and knew she had surrendered. Knew that she wanted exactly what he wanted in this hot moment that had progressed so quickly beyond her innocence, and beyond his thought, his reason.

He pulled away from the roaring flame of his own desire. It took every ounce of his strength. If he was going to return her to her world unscathed, then it was imperative he not consummate this marriage. That he be able to quietly seek an annulment so that her name and her life would not be damaged.

He got out of the bed, and looked into the hurt and bewilderment in her eyes.

Someday, she would thank him for walking away from what she had just offered.

But not really offered to *him*, he reminded himself, as he went across the room to his own room and closed the door behind him.

A prince. She knew he had ridden up on his white steed and rescued her. She had just offered him something in return. Payment.

Payment.

He felt sick. He stripped off his rumpled clothes, leaving on only his boxers and climbed into his bed, which seemed too large and too empty. After a long time he went to sleep.

He woke to the sound of Carly laughing. He got up and

pulled on his pants and peeked through into Rachel's room. The baby was playing with a huge stuffed bear that was at the foot of the crib, and laughing uproariously. Rachel's pantsuit was now in a rumpled heap on the floor, and he could see a delectable length of naked leg among the tumble of blankets. But her head was buried under a pillow, and she did not wake up.

"Morning, princess," he whispered to Carly, tiptoeing into the room.

"Uppie," she crowed.

He did as commanded, taking her and the stuffed bear. He took them out of her mother's room so Rachel could sleep, and put Carly on his bed. He took the bear and made it hop across the bed to her. He had it nuzzle her cheek, and then said in a deep bearlike growl, "You taste like cookie dough."

Carly gurgled.

"I love cookie dough," he said in the same voice, and had the bear pretend to lick her while he made enormous slurping sounds. Carly roared with laughter, and slapped at the bear.

"Is there any cookie dough between your toes?" he asked in his bear voice.

"Nooo," Carly shouted.

But the bear checked anyway, slurping loudly.

"Yes, there is!" he cried. "I found cookie dough between your toes!" More slurping noises, which Carly obviously adored.

"Is there any cookie dough in your...belly button?"

"Nooo!" Carly shrieked.

But the bear banged his head impolitely against her tummy, making loud sniffing and snuffling noises.

"I'm sure I smell cookie dough," the bear said slowly.

"Sniff, sniff, here it is! It's not in your belly button at all! It's in your ear!"

Carly batted at the bear, shrieking with delight.

And then he became aware that Rachel was standing in the doorway in a rumpled camisole and plaid boxer shorts that had Bugs Bunny on them. Her hair was a wild tangle, her eyes smudged, her legs long and sexy, the camisole just a wee bit see-through.

"Oh, look," he said in his best bear voice, "there's Mama bear. Do you think she has any cookie dough on her?"

"Yesss!" Carly howled.

He took the bear and held it up in front of him. "I'm looking for cookie dough," he warned.

"There's none on me!" Rachel said, backing away from him.

"You must never run away from a hungry bear," he told her.

She ran, and he and the bear chased her, while Carly howled with hilarity. Rachel hopped up over the bed and bounced Carly, followed by Damon who bounced her even harder.

"I smell cookie dough," he proclaimed, as he followed the fleet Rachel around the bedroom again. "I'm sure I do."

"No, you don't," Rachel gasped. "You do not. Damon!"

"My name's not Damon. My name is Bernie the Bear."

"Bernie the Bear, you do not smell cookie dough!"

Laughing, she tripped and fell on his bed.

He brought the bear close to her face, and made sniffing noises.

She choked with laughter.

The bear sniffed her hair. "No cookie dough there. Carly, where is the cookie dough?"

"Nose!" Carly screeched.

The bear obediently sniffed. "Nope, it's not there, Carly."

"Toes," Carly suggested hysterically.

The bear obediently went down to Rachel's toes. Rachel tried to squirm away, but Damon had a free hand, and he caught her ankle and held her.

"Yessir, here it is," he said, and made loud chomping noises, while tickling Rachel's feet with the bear.

It occurred to him he was happy. Simply and ridiculously happy. Rachel was screaming with laughter now, begging him to stop, which, of course, only made his search for cookie dough more intense.

And then there was a loud and imperious knock on the door.

Rachel's eyes went very round. She mouthed "Who?" and he shrugged.

"Yes?" he called.

The door flew open and his mother stood there, diminutive and regal, already dressed for the day in a very proper tweed suit.

He looked at Rachel, who was trying to crawl under the covers. He realized he was naked from the waist up and that it all looked very naughty and improper.

He laughed out loud.

"Damon," his mother said, "I understand you have guests."

"Yes, I do," he said easily. He scooped Carly up, tossed her in the air, and then cradled her in the crook of his arm and went over to his mother.

"I want you to meet Carly," he said.

His mother glared at him, tried to smile at the baby,

looked over at Rachel, who had now only the top part of her nose and her eyes visible from under the sheets.

"What is going on, Damon?" his mother asked in a loud whisper.

"I got married yesterday," he answered in an equally loud whisper.

He couldn't believe how free it made him feel to say it.

His mother stared at him. Out of the corner of his eye he saw Rachel disappear the rest of the way under the sheets.

"Married?" his mother echoed.

"Married," he repeated firmly.

Her mouth worked soundlessly, she sputtered a few times, and then she turned on her heel and walked out of the room, shutting the door behind her.

He looked over at the sheets. They were trembling.

He went and yanked them back. Rachel was sputtering with laughter. He began to laugh, too, and so did Carly. He picked up the bear. "Now about that cookie dough."

"Oh, Damon," Rachel said, "thank you."

"I should be thanking you," he said in his bear voice. "I have never tasted such delicious cookie dough." And in his normal voice, he said, "Sweet Rachel, what are you thanking me for?"

"I needed to laugh. I feel so upset about my sister, and maybe it's awful to laugh when she's missing, but I needed to more than anything else."

"I understand that," he said. The bear nudged Carly, who giggled.

"Would you like for her to call you Daddy?" Rachel asked shyly.

It felt then as if his whole world tilted. He, too, had just needed to laugh, to play. But now reality was back.

He knew what she was offering. Everything. Everything she had and was. But he was going to have to let them go as soon as he got them through this. It would only hurt them all the more if certain things happened.

Like that beautiful baby calling him Daddy.

His heart yearned for it.

He hardened it, and said, "Maybe not just yet."

And then he had to turn away from the bewildered hurt in Rachel's face. Twice now he'd hurt her. Last night, when he had turned away from the invitation of her lips, understanding better than she did that her motives were wrong, and again now.

The phone rang, and he answered it and listened, then hung up and turned to Rachel.

"We have just had a royal summons. Would you care to join my parents for breakfast?"

"Do I have a choice?" Rachel said. "What a terrible first impression I've made. She must have heard me shrieking! Good grief, I'm in my underwear."

"It serves her right for barging in without an invitation."

"Does she do that often?" Rachel asked, distressed.

"She's never done it before. It must have been the sound of people having fun that brought her on the double."

"Is that such an uncommon sound here?" Rachel asked.

"Not anymore," he said, and then fully felt the sadness in him. Because it would not be for long. If he gave himself over to the joyous celebration of them being in his life, would it only hurt more when he said goodbye?

He decided, suddenly, he didn't care. He had been given the gift of these two incredible people in his life, and he would accept that gift, no matter what the cost when he had to let go.

"Are you up to breakfast?"

Rachel made a face. "Where's the nearest McDonald's?"

He smiled. "Thortonburg."

Carly announced, "Breadie now."

Rachel laughed. "I guess that settles it. On to the royal dining room. Damon?"

"Yes, my love?" The words came out unrehearsed, and for a moment they both froze in the power of them.

Rachel got up off the bed. "What do I wear?"

"Whatever you want. I'm wearing jeans."

She didn't wear jeans, though. Somehow she had to erase the impression she had made this morning, her hair tousled, her cheeks flushed, in her Bugs Bunny shorts! What would his mother think?

So she dressed in a gray linen pantsuit that was beautiful and elegant and boring, and pulled her hair back and fastened it with a clip that was also beautiful and elegant and boring. When she looked in the mirror, she looked very proper. Did the sadness show in her eyes?

This morning, caught in the wonder of the moment, playing with him and Carly, she had almost forgotten his rejection of her last night. But it was right there in her eyes. A pain that was different than any pain she had ever gone through before. Different than when she had finally pulled her head out of the sand to recognize Bryan's true colors, different than the kind of pain she felt over her mother dying, and her sister being missing, and her father's treachery.

Not deeper, only different.

She noticed boxes at the base of the crib and opened one. Inside was a lovely little pinafore dress for Carly—

white ruffled apron, puffy red-checked sleeves, and a full ruffled skirt.

"Where did this come from?" she asked Damon, coming through the shared bathroom into his bedroom.

True to his word he was in jeans and a light brown brushed suede shirt that made his eyes seem more gold than green.

He glanced at her, and then looked quickly away, but not before she saw what he did not want her to see. A flame of desire had lit in his eyes.

But if that was true, why had he said no to her last night?

He was leaning his back against the head of his bed, his long legs stretched out over the mattress. Carly was in the crook of his arm, pointing imperiously at pictures in the paper.

"That's a space shuttle," he said patiently.

"Pace buttle," Carly repeated obediently.

"I bought a few things for her."

"When did you find time to do that?"

He took sudden interest in the paper. "That's a prize-winning Hanoverian stallion," he told Carly intently.

Carly smacked him on the arm. "Horsey," she corrected him.

"Horsey," he agreed. "Phillip went shopping. I think he enjoyed it immensely."

She didn't understand him. He obviously planned to be the doting daddy in every way, except one. He didn't want to be called Daddy.

It had hurt her terribly when he had said that. She had offered it to him as her only remaining gift, and he had said no. What could she give the man who had everything?

But he had refused both her gifts now, and in his refusal

Rachel had seen that perhaps he felt he had made a mistake, after all.

She felt torn—as if she wanted to hop on the bed and look at the paper with him, while also needing to protect herself from him.

"I'll just take Carly and pop her into this dress," she said stiffly.

He surrendered Carly reluctantly, and Carly went, howling her dismay. "Weed," she told her mother, pointing frantically at the paper.

"I thought you were hungry," Rachel reminded her.

"Oh." With one last longing look at the paper, and her new playmate, Carly allowed herself to be carried away and put in the dress, which she admired at length in front of the bathroom mirror.

When they were ready, Damon led them all down to the dining room, a monstrous affair with a huge table, a gigantic chandelier hanging over its polished surface. A heavy sideboard held a feast of bacon and sausages and eggs and toast and waffles and fresh fruits.

Damon's parents arrived.

"I understand I have a new daughter-in-law," Charles said. If he was surprised or dismayed, neither emotion showed on his well-schooled features as he was introduced to Rachel. When he was introduced to Carly, Rachel caught the first true glimpse of Damon's nature in him, for he smiled with unconcealed delight.

"Better than Christmas," he proclaimed to his wife, who looked largely unconvinced. "To wake up and find oneself a grandparent."

Damon presented Rachel formally to his mother, introducing his mother as Princess Nora of Roxbury. Her grip seemed distant and her gaze icy and disapproving as she shook Rachel's hand.

But Damon's father's remark allowed Rachel to start breathing again. A servant, actually dressed in a uniform of a gray skirt and white apron and a cap, came and asked her what she could get Carly for breakfast. Somehow Rachel couldn't help feeling that life had probably qualified her more for that servant's position than the one she now held. Glancing once more at her formidable mother-in-law's face, she couldn't help but feel she would have found agreement in that corner.

"Rachel, you must tell us about yourself," Princess Nora insisted when they were all settled in with heaping platters of food.

Carly was throwing hers on the floor, delighting in the young serving girl's efforts to keep up with her. Damon's father was laughing into his napkin.

Rachel kept it short and sweet—that she was the daughter of a headmaster, a single mother, and a technical writer. That she had met Damon after returning to Thortonburg after a long absence.

Of course, the inevitable question was asked. "How did you meet?"

Damon stepped in. "An act of God," he said smoothly.

His mother looked from one to the other and then sighed. "I'll need to do an official announcement, of course. And there will be a party. Rachel, I don't suppose you've had much experience dealing with the press, have you?"

"No, I—"

"Then we'll bring in that consultant. Do you remember her name, Damon, the one—"

"Mother, for a number of reasons, Rachel and I have decided not to go public with our marriage just yet. And when we do, Rachel will be fine just the way she is."

A simple statement, but one Rachel needed to hear. It

changed something in her, reminded her of who she really was. Whether she was a serving girl or a princess, she knew her own heart. She knew she was a good person. She knew she was honest. And hardworking. She knew she lived to a standard of integrity not everyone would understand. She knew she had a wonderful sense of humor. And she knew, most of all, that when the moment called for it, she had resources of courage within her. She had had the courage to say yes to having a baby even though it meant facing the world alone, and losing the approval of her father, and she had done it anyway, done exactly what her heart told her was right to do.

Somehow, ever since meeting Damon, her sense of who she was had been getting lost in the excitement and the confusion.

But it felt as though it was back now.

"But, Damon," his mother said, "you can't very well share quarters without an explanation. That could place you in an awkward situation. It is bound to get out."

"I don't see why. Our staff has always been loyal to us to the extreme. It won't be forever, anyway, Mother, just for a while."

"But why?"

"I can tell you only that it is literally a matter of life or death. That is all I can divulge."

His mother shot Rachel a perturbed look, as if she had personally brought the possibility of scandal to this quiet island, where scandal was avoided at all costs, but she met the look with quiet dignity, not accepting the judgment in Nora's eyes.

"Damon—"

But it was his father who held up his hand. "My dearest Nora," he said, "Damon is an adult. He has always behaved with responsibility beyond his years. He has asked us to trust him, and I for one am quite willing to do that.''

When Nora looked at her husband, something softened in her features, and she demurred quickly, saying, ''Of course, you're right.''

''Now, if breakfast is done, I need to steal Damon away from his honeymoon for just a few minutes. We have to iron out some of the details regarding Thorton Shipping. Do you mind?'' he asked Rachel.

She was delighted that he had asked, and knew where Damon got his old world manners from, but of course she was not at all delighted at the prospect of being left with Damon's mother.

Still, she nodded, knowing it was a test of her self-worth that she had to pass, a test that she was going to be given again and again.

The same maid was now wiping Carly's face, or trying to, which meant that Rachel didn't even have motherly duties to hide behind.

So instead she faced Princess Nora squarely, and said, ''We would have told you last night, but we had an emergency in Thortonburg and didn't get in until late.''

She could tell by the look on the princess's face that she did not approve of emergencies.

''I am very sorry if we shocked you this morning,'' Rachel said.

Nora looked at her for a long moment. Then, surprisingly, she shooed away the maid, and took the cloth from her, firmly wiping Carly's face where the baby had managed to outwit the maid.

Then she set down the cloth and extracted Carly from the high chair.

''She's a lovely child,'' Princess Nora said. ''Charles was right. A gift to us.''

"Thank you," Rachel said, seeing the first hints of softening in the face across from her.

"You knew about Damon's wife and baby?"

"Yes, he told me. A terrible tragedy."

Princess Nora bounced Carly experimentally on one tweedy knee. "There have been times when I wondered if I would ever hear him laugh again." She looked up at Rachel. "I heard him laughing this morning, through the door."

It was a white flag, and Rachel recognized it as the beginning of being accepted by her new mother-in-law.

"Being a royal parent is very hard, a balance between love and duty, responsibility to your subjects, responsibility to yourself, responsibility to your family."

Was it a welcome or a warning?

Princess Nora held her gaze. "But in her heart, what every mother always wants more than anything else is for her children to be happy." She sighed. "You seem to have given Damon that, and I thank you. But you should know that being a member of a royal family is not all about fairy tales."

"I didn't marry Damon because he was part of a royal family," Rachel said. "I would have married him if he was a bricklayer."

Damon's mother raised her eyebrows at her. "Why did you marry him then? Frankly, it would seem you hardly knew him."

"I guess that's why," Rachel said. "My head said it hardly knew him, and my heart said it had known him for all time." She pondered her own words for a moment, and found them rich with truth. Her truth. It did not matter who else it was true for.

Damon came back into the room just then.

"Rachel," he said, "we need to talk. I've just heard from Lance Grayson."

Rachel shot up out of her seat, excused herself to Princess Nora as she reclaimed the baby, then tucked Carly into her hip and followed Damon from the room.

"What is it?" she asked.

He turned to her and took her shoulders between his hands. "A second ransom note has just been delivered to the Thortons."

Chapter Eight

"What have they asked for?" Rachel asked.

He found himself in awe of her quiet strength. She took this latest blow without flinching.

"One million. But there's good news, Rachel. There was a picture of Victoria holding this morning's newspaper."

"She's alive then, at least."

"Yes. And according to Grayson, looks unharmed. There was no sign at all that she had been abused. In fact, his words were that she looked fighting mad."

"That's my sister."

"Grayson has asked for your help. The note was handwritten this time, and he's sending it over with a special messenger right away to see if you recognize the handwriting."

"If it's my father's, I'll be able to identify it. I hope it's not. I'm afraid Princess Nora would react badly to having a kidnapper in her family as an in-law. I hope with all my heart that my father is in no way involved in this—

that he is as he had always appeared to be, a crabby, but respectable headmaster.''

"It is no reflection on you how your father behaves."

"I know that now."

"Good. Grayson is sending the photo as well. He wants you to look at the background detail and see if it might be a place you recognize."

"He knows his job, doesn't he?" she asked.

"Inside and out," Damon agreed. "He struck me as a man who simply will not accept defeat. Ever. He also said the drop-off spot for the money has been named. He wondered if that might mean anything to you."

"Where is it?"

"A park in the Mulberry neighborhood of Thortonburg. There are several routes into it, and it's heavily treed. There are tennis courts, a duck pond, and a children's play area in the park."

"That area of Thortonburg is old and going to seed just a little bit. My father was snobby in the oddest ways. Mulberry was not on his list of places he took us. Actually, the places he took us would make quite a short list."

She said this without any kind of reproach or self-pity, but Damon felt his dislike of his father-in-law grow. To have two beautiful children and to make them seem as though they weren't worth his time, as though he did not enjoy them, seemed to Damon like the worst of crimes. He also noted that Rachel seemed relieved that her father didn't favor the Mulberry area, but Damon personally thought that if he had committed this crime, he would deliberately make the drop-off area a place he was not known to go.

He could see that familiar knot of worry forming on her brow, and thought again of the reasons he had given himself for marrying her. That he would look after her and protect her. Now that he knew he would set her free as soon as her difficulties were over, it seemed imperative that he give her gifts now that she had never had before.

His time. A chance to be carefree. To have some joy. With her sister missing, giving these things to her would be a challenge. He thought of how he would feel if it was Lily missing, how he would lose his mind if he just sat and helplessly pondered her predicament. So it seemed more important than ever to take Rachel's mind off her difficulties, to divert her as much as he could.

And he admitted to himself that he was getting better at not entirely keeping himself in the dark as to the nature of his motives, because giving her the gift of his time would also be giving a gift to himself.

Brother Raymond came to mind again—or, more precisely—one of his one-liners that Damon found infinitely irritating until he gave them some thought, and then it seemed they held truth in them, truth spelled out in very simple and clear terms.

Brother Raymond was always telling him to live one day at a time. To immerse himself in the moment—to find peace in the perfection of a single leaf on a tree, the high lilting notes of a bird song, the ever-changing color of the sky.

"Miracles," his plump friend would tell him, "are all around us all the time."

And when Damon looked at Rachel, that was what he saw. A miracle of loveliness and strength that he wanted to explore while he had the chance.

"We left Carly yesterday," he said. "Why don't we spend the day with her today? We can go down to the beach. Even though it's unusually hot today, the water is probably still a bit too cold for swimming, but it will be wonderful for wading. And I'm a master at sand castles."

"Sand castles?" she said skeptically.

He could see the worry knot let go just a little bit.

"Remember juggling," he told her.

And he was rewarded when she laughed.

"Damon, I'd love to, but maybe I should stay here. Just in case..."

"I'll bring the cell phone with us, and as soon as Grayson's messenger arrives, I'll have him sent to the beach."

"I can't resist you," she said.

He thought of her inviting him with her lips last night. Did she mean it in more ways than one?

An avenue he could not allow his mind to go down as much as it wanted to.

He had been right, Rachel thought, as she watched him at the water's edge with Carly. Carly was perched on his shoulders, and he was barefoot and had his jeans rolled up at the knees and was leaping waves.

The sun felt so good on her cheeks, and his laughter and Carly's eased something in her that felt desperate and keyed up and helpless.

She felt as though she should be doing something. Putting up posters on streetlamps, knocking on doors with her sister's photo, asking people if they had seen her. And yet she knew she had to trust those like Lance Grayson who knew what they were doing. A wrong move on her part would endanger her sister rather than help her.

She was wearing her new bathing suit, and the matching sarong. She thought she was probably the most superficial person in the world to still care what she looked like, even as her sister was being held captive somewhere.

Damon returned and swung Carly down from his shoulders and dropped in the sand beside Rachel. The look in his eyes, though quickly veiled, made her glad she had worn the bathing suit. He had brought an enormous array of containers, cheerfully carting them down the trail that led from the castle to the beach. The trail was beautiful, parts of it so steep that stairways had been carved right in the stone. The beach, too, was gorgeous, a crescent of golden sand at the foot of formidable cliffs.

Now Damon rummaged through his collection and found a blue plastic bucket and shovels. Together, he and Carly filled the bucket with the semi-wet sand where the tide had gone out, Carly patting the sand officiously with the flat side of her shovel. When he swiftly turned the bucket over and slid it off the sand, Carly's eyes grew round. She wrenched the bucket from his grasp and began eagerly refilling it.

Damon smiled at her, and then at Rachel. "Do you suppose children are put here to remind us there is magic in the smallest of things?"

She looked at him watching her daughter, and thought how terribly easy it would be to love him. But maybe half her problem in life was that she did find it too terribly easy to love people. Bryan being a classic example.

Damon passed her a pail of her own. "Everyone on this construction site works," he told her firmly. "No loafers."

She suspected he was trying to get her mind off the grim matters at hand, and she felt thankful to him for it. She took the pail.

"That pail makes the shape that goes where I am marking these Xs."

Rachel complied, feeling a surprising sense of well-being overtake her anxiety as she performed her simple task of filling buckets.

"I think your design is a little grandiose," she told him after several minutes of trying to keep up with his Xs.

"Grandiose?" he said with such heartfelt shock that she had to laugh. "Who is the prince here?"

"You are, Your Royal Highness," she said, her humility somewhat damaged by her giggle.

"An authority on castles," he reminded her sternly. "Carly!"

Rachel saw that Carly had been following her, diligently smashing each of her carefully placed sand towers. She laughed and so did Carly.

Damon pretended to scowl at them. He gave Carly a stern lecture. She put a handful of golden sand in her mouth and chewed it thoughtfully while she listened.

"Here, Carly, you help Mommy fill the buckets. No more smashing things, or Damon will pick you up and toss you in the sea for the serpents to eat."

Carly laughed recklessly at that. But she stopped smashing things.

Rachel, watching the sand castle take definite shape, thought of her mother. How Maribelle had loved the beach. Rachel realized it was one of the few places she had seen her mother laugh and smile. It seemed to her that on the beach Maribelle had always looked beautiful, not sad or broken. She could recall her mother standing at the water's edge, looking out with a faraway look on her face, building sand castles with her and Victoria with a childlike enthusiasm she usually did not have, her rare laughter making her girls smile with delight.

It struck Rachel that Maribelle and Malcolm's relationship had been largely devoid of laughter, of any kind of joy, or even contentment.

In light of the information that Rachel now had about Victoria, she wondered about that. When had her mother stopped smiling? When had Malcolm become so domineering, so hard to please, so mean-spirited? It had never occurred to Rachel that these qualities might not have been so much inherent to her parent's individual natures, as to their relationship.

"Sandlady, you are daydreaming," Damon said in her ear. "There are Xs that require your undivided attention."

"Aye, aye, sir," she said. Carly was now engaged in the serious business of digging a hole, and Rachel wished her mother could have had just one day with her granddaughter on the beach like this.

But then, who knew how these things really worked? Maybe her mother was as much here now as she had ever been. Her broken spirit finally free.

"What are you thinking?" Damon asked.

"I'm thinking of how my mother would have enjoyed a day like this. I'm wondering if she's here in some way. I'm sure her idea of heaven would have been a beach."

Damon touched Rachel's hair, pushed a few wind-tangled strands behind her ear. "Of course she's here," he said. "I think what's best about her has gone on, in you and in Carly."

What was best about her mother? Her beauty, of course, and her gentleness, which had, thanks to Malcolm, eventually deteriorated into weakness. Why had her parents gotten together? Had they not had the sense to see what a mismatch it was? Her father, homely, cut from the cloth of Ichabod Crane, so much older, and her mother a breathless beauty? Her mother a gentle dreamer and her father a pragmatic taskmaster whose pragmatism had eventually given way to harshness?

When had her parents gotten together? It occurred to her those photo albums that she had taken from her cottage at the last minute might provide a clue.

"We need a moat," Damon told her, handing her a spade.

She broke out of her daydreams to see that Carly had given up on digging to Asia and was now attempting to haul water in her bucket. She was sitting at the edge of the waves, yelling orders at the water to get in her tipped bucket. The water was not cooperating. She tried scooping some in with her shovel. Finally, she seemed to have captured a few drops, and crowing victory she came back toward them. But her walking skills, limited at best, were even more challenged in the sand, and she fell and lost her treasure before she made it back to them.

"She's no quitter," Damon commented, watching Carly march back to the water's edge.

Keeping a watchful eye on Carly, Rachel built a moat around his castle. It was quite an unbelievable structure. It was as high as her waist in places, with simple turrets and wings and walls.

"You truly are an expert on castles," she conceded, making a mock bow at him.

"The best is yet to come," he told her.

"And what's that?"

"We wreck it."

"No!"

"If we don't, the tide will."

So, almost as soon as they were done building it, they let Carly begin to kick it down, and then Rachel found herself in there, thoroughly enjoying the destruction.

As she did her last gleeful leap in the sand, she saw a young man coming down the beach toward them.

There was something about him that she found quite arresting, and it was more than his chiseled good looks, dark hair, and blue eyes. He was very tall, and not dressed for the beach at all, but rather looked ready to go riding.

She glanced at Damon. "Who is that?" she asked, thinking the young man looked vaguely familiar.

"Roland Thorton."

She gasped, because for the first time she knew truly that Victoria was the grand duke's daughter.

"He looks unbelievably like Victoria," she said, as the young man approached them, graceful despite the sand sucking at his feet.

"Damon," the younger man said.

"Roland."

Something softened in Roland's eyes as he turned to her. "And you must be Rachel, my sister's sister. I wonder what that makes us to each other?"

She smiled, liking him instantly. "I don't know," she admitted.

"I've brought you some things from Lance to look at."

"Thank you."

His smile fell away. "Rachel, I'm sorry about your sister. And mine. I truly am hoping for an outcome that brings us all joy."

"Thank you."

"I've only seen the photographs of her," Roland said, "and I've suspected they don't do her justice. Is she as beautiful as you?"

Something made her glance at Damon again. His brow had furrowed downward, and he looked unbelievably, unmistakably jealous.

"She looks just like you," Rachel told Roland.

"I can't wait to meet her, and I mean that with all my heart."

"Go find Lily," Damon snapped.

Roland saluted them casually and walked back up the sand.

"Be nice," Rachel said, "he's going to be your brother-in-law. Besides, he's very attractive and charming.

Your not being female, you may not have picked up on his many irresistible qualities.''

"Irresistible?" Damon sputtered. "May I remind you, you are a married woman?"

She smiled at that, but studied him thoughtfully. There was something wrong with this picture. He had refused her kisses. And said he was not ready to have Carly call him Daddy. And yet the look in his eyes right now was hot and passionate. And the man he had been on the beach all day had been a perfect daddy.

She wanted to throw herself at him, but did not think she could bear it if he pushed her away again.

So instead she sat down on the blanket on the beach, and opened the envelope Roland had given her. Damon brought Carly up from the edge of the sea, and planted her firmly at Rachel's feet with her bucket, and then sat down beside Rachel.

Out of the corner of her eye, she could see sand tangled in the dark, shining hair of his forearms, and for some reason it struck her as almost unbearably sexy.

She forced herself to focus on the photocopy of the ransom note that she had been sent.

It was with relief that she realized she did not recognize the handwriting. "It's not my father's handwriting," she said, passing Damon the note. "It's not even his composition. He wouldn't make spelling mistakes or grammatical errors like that."

"I don't think anyone thinks he pulled it off by himself."

Actually, the thought of an accomplice had not occurred to her, and she realized her relief about the note was probably premature.

Damon studied the note, but didn't comment further,

except to say he didn't think a professional crook would have sent a handwritten note.

She looked now at the photograph of her sister, ran her fingers gently over those familiar high cheekbones, ached for the terror and uncertainty Victoria must be feeling. Not that there was any terror or uncertainty in Victoria's face.

Lance Grayson's description had been totally accurate. Victoria, rather than looking like a frightened victim, looked fighting mad.

And then Rachel forced herself to focus on the details of the background, which were shadowy. The picture must have been taken with a flash, Victoria's face starkly white, the background quite dark. But a further investigation of the envelope showed that Lance had provided several photos where the background was enhanced.

It looked as if her sister was standing in front of a wall. An unusual wall, constructed of logs.

"A cabin?" Damon guessed, looking over her shoulder.

In the far right-hand corner of the photo an object had been circled in red. Rachel peered at it, and moved to the next photo which was another blowup, this time of the object.

"It looks like an antique rifle or something, doesn't it?" Damon asked.

"I hope it works," Rachel said with feeling, "and that Victoria gets her hands on it, and—"

She stopped herself. It wasn't a movie, after all.

She looked through all the photographs again, very slowly and carefully. Something about them made her feel as if she should know this spot, but she didn't. Her father had never taken them on holidays as a family. The odd day trip had been to the museum, the zoo, the grounds of the Thortonburg castle.

"Well?" Damon asked.

"I don't know," Rachel said. "It seems like I should know something, but I don't. Maybe I just want so badly to help, my mind is telling me this place seems familiar in some vague way, but at the same time I know for a fact I've never been there."

"How about when you were very young?"

Rachel looked at it again, felt her mind bending under the strain. "No," she said. "I've never been there. I guess I just wish I had been." Reluctantly she put the pictures away. "I think we need to get Carly out of the sun now. She'll be needing a nap soon, and she does a wonderful impression of Dr. Jekyll and Mr. Hyde when that doesn't happen right on time."

"I'm going to have to leave you for a while. I have several pressing business matters that I dare not neglect any longer."

"Oh, Damon, I hope you weren't neglecting your business affairs for us! We're quite capable of entertaining ourselves."

"I wouldn't have missed this day for the earth."

Rachel realized she could make good use of her time alone by going through those old photo albums, looking for clues of who her family had really been, which she suspected was a long way from what she had assumed they always were.

But more than it being about nostalgia, maybe there was something in those old albums that would help her think where Victoria might be.

They packed up the baby, the blanket, the buckets, and found the steep trail going up the cliffs.

Carly took her place on Damon's shoulders, and he groaned and said, "I'll be glad when she's old enough to ride a horse."

Rachel stopped to look at him and the picture he made with her daughter high on his shoulders, and she felt as if it was a scene from a dream she had once had for herself, a long, long time ago, when she was a little girl and still believed in dreams.

"Thank you," she told him.

"For?" he asked.

"For being my perfect prince." Even as she said it, she felt dread. She was old enough to know fairy tales did not come true. She had been in the same house with her mother and father long enough to learn a bitter truth. Good things did not last.

Damon left them unwillingly, but he knew he had work to catch up on. He was plowing his way through a ton of backlogged paperwork when Phillip came in.

"Sir, I looked after your wife's—" Phillip's enjoyment of Damon's new marital status was evident in the way he said *wife's* "—bills as you requested. But one of them wasn't a bill. I'm afraid I opened it in error."

"Not your fault, Phillip. What was it?"

Phillip passed it to him, and Damon scanned it quickly and then read it again more slowly. What he wanted to do, his first base instinct, was to ball up the letter and put it in the garbage.

The letter was from a publisher of children's books. They wanted to buy Rachel's story, and to pursue the possibility of making it into a series.

Phillip was grinning at him. "Isn't that wonderful, sir?"

"Wonderful," he agreed without feeling it. Phillip left, and he looked again at the letter, indulging in his mixed feelings.

He had rescued a woman who didn't need rescuing at all.

Really, it was an insult to her. By marrying her he might as well have said to her he didn't think she was capable of making it on her own.

And according to this letter she was more than capable.

That part of him that was in all men, that was self-centered and controlling, still wanted to put the letter in the garbage.

Because what it really meant to him, was that the time had come much sooner than he thought to let her go.

He sighed and rubbed his temples. He could almost feel Brother Raymond smiling. Brother Raymond would say what he was about to do was about true love, pure love.

Putting what he wanted, and needed, on hold, and going to her and setting her free. Giving her wings, showing her that he believed she could fly.

He looked at the letter again, and put it aside, knowing he would have to show it to her as soon as possible. Maybe, like their day on the beach, it would divert her from her sister's dilemma for a moment, allow her joy. What kind of man would he be not to want that for her?

A time was going to come when it was right to tell her that their marriage was over. That he was sorry, but he felt they should seek an annulment before she and Carly were so involved that it would be hard to get out without a deluge of negative publicity.

He thought of Rachel the way she had looked today in that gorgeous black and red bathing suit, the silk sarong hiding her delectable legs. He thought of Carly comically toddling along the beach with those half buckets of water.

Quietly he went out of his office.

Rachel was in her room, and if he was not mistaken, through the door he heard her crying. Trapped here in a life she had not freely chosen. That she had agreed to because she was so innately good—because she had thought it would help him, and help her daughter.

He slipped by their bedrooms and went down to the next door.

He opened it and went inside.

The nursery seemed empty and sad, like a mirror of what his life was about to become again.

He went over and touched the crib, and found that oddly he had gone, in just a few short days, from believing he never wanted another child, to aching for one.

For a moment something wild rose in him, and he thought of going to Rachel and seducing her. Taking her up on her invitation of last night, making this marriage so much harder for her to escape.

He realized it would be more like hostage taking than lovemaking. He couldn't do it to her.

She had said to him once she thought he was more in prison than she was.

And how right she had been.

So what had he done? Opened the prison door for her to join him in the cell. Invited her into a world where her every move would be scrutinized and her daughter would be photographed every time she had an ice-cream cone in public, where they would have to learn to watch the angle of the sun when they wore summer dresses, because some photographer would be waiting for them to make a mistake, expose themselves.

It had started as a business agreement, he thought. And in terms of business, perhaps it had not been such a bad idea.

But something had changed all that.

Love.

He had fallen in love with his beautiful young wife. In

the blink of an eye, really, she had taken his wounded heart and worked a miracle on it.

He allowed himself to think for a moment what it would be like to love her and live with her according to the vows they had made.

To have children together.

To play together.

To work together, doing what was in their power to make the world a better place.

He suddenly envied Lillian and Roland. They came from the same world. They could make it work.

And he wished for all the world he and Rachel could, too.

Chapter Nine

Rachel sniffled and reached for yet another tissue. She should have known the bathing suit had been a mistake. In her attempts to be alluring on the beach today, she seemed to have caught a terrible cold.

Well, she certainly looked alluring now, with her red nose and running eyes. But the one she wanted to look alluring for was nowhere to be seen anyway.

She found her photo albums, and went to the oldest one, the one her mother had given her when she moved away. It seemed it was becoming frail in its old age. A paper slipped out even as she lifted it away from the others. She tucked it carefully back among the pages, and took the heavy album to a comfy armchair tucked between Carly's crib and her bed, and settled the book on her lap. The very first page was Victoria's baby picture, a glossy eight-by-ten, faded somewhat now. Rachel realized it really didn't prove anything, except that Victoria had once been a baby.

The album did its best to present a picture of a happy

and harmonious family. There were pictures of picnics and birthday parties and anniversaries. But when Rachel looked closely, it seemed to her she could now see that the unhappiness between her parents had always been there. Something aloof in her father's eyes as he looked at the camera, and something desperate and pleading in her mother's. Even when they stood side by side holding their brand-new baby, Victoria.

But in light of all the new things she had learned, she knew they also might have lied about Victoria for all the reasons people lie about these things—to protect their own dignity, to make their child's way easier through life.

One thread that did run like gold through the book were the pictures of Rachel and Victoria together. Nearly always laughing, always holding hands, always a team, in a home that would have been unbearably cold had they not warmed themselves on the fire of each other's love.

There they were in the back garden on a chilly fall day in matching little red jackets, the hoods trimmed with white fake fur, Victoria leaping in the leaves that Rachel had worked so hard to rake.

There they were, in identical polka-dot bathing suits, playing in the round, plastic pool they filled with water in the summer. Victoria was dumping a bucket of water over Rachel's head.

There they were, a little older now, hanging from their knees from the top bar of the swing set, Victoria laughing, Rachel looking terrified.

There they were, ready for church, in little navy blue suits with white gloves and hats, Victoria sticking out her tongue and crossing her eyes, and Rachel looking so prim and proper.

There they were, holding an uncooperative Taffy, Ginger's predecessor, in their baby doll carriage, the poor puppy trying to wriggle out of the sweater and bonnet Victoria had insisted it wear.

And there they were, chasing that same dog, older now, around the yard, the dog with Victoria's brand-new two-piece bathing suit top caught between his sharp little teeth.

Rachel sighed, realizing how deeply she missed her sister, realizing how much she needed to undo the angry words that had passed between them about Bryan, and say the words her heart needed to say. *Victoria, I love you.*

Pride had stopped her. The residue of pain.

And now she might never have a chance.

What a terrible way to learn this lesson—that the words *I love you* needed to be spoken now.

She turned the page again, and came to the piece of paper that had fluttered to the floor only moments ago. It was yellow with age, worn along the fold lines.

Carefully, Rachel unfolded it, flattened it out with the palm of her hand. And found her mother and father's marriage certificate.

The dates were all as she remembered them, except one. This document said her parents had been married a year later than they had always publicly proclaimed. Which meant that Victoria had been born *after* they had been married. Six months after they had been married, to be exact.

So, only one question really remained.

Had Malcolm known that when he had married her mother? That she was pregnant with another man's child? Had he known and offered his protection and care?

The blood drained from her face as she recognized an eerie parallel to her own situation.

Except that Malcolm was no Damon. At least not in her memory. But had he been once? A long time ago?

Had he, once upon a time, perceived himself as rescuing a damsel in distress? She found it hard to imagine.

The other possibility seemed just as unlikely. That her sweet mother had been capable of enough duplicity to marry a man without revealing to him she was pregnant. According to the dates on this license, she would have been three months along, far enough to know beyond a shadow of a doubt of her condition.

What had it meant that Maribelle had named her daughter after the man who had not married her, a man of incredible stature in their community, a man who was married to someone else? That she loved the grand duke and needed to keep some part of that love alive inside her?

It had been so easy, when they were growing up, to always see Malcolm as cold and heartless, and yet it seemed now as if maybe her mother had played her own role in that. Malcolm was not a stupid man. How long had it taken him to figure out his beautiful young wife's heart did not belong to him?

Rachel thought of the special tenderness her mother had always reserved for Victoria, a tenderness that Rachel had ached to share, but had been excluded from despite her mother's surface efforts to always treat them the same.

But she had felt her father's favor. Because, she saw, she was *his*.

She did not know if she had the story right, but she suspected she was coming close to unraveling the dark secrets that had made her childhood home such an unhappy place. She did not feel any condemnation at all for her mother. Maribelle had likely been penniless and desperate, and when Malcolm had come by with a life raft she had scrambled on board.

Uneasily, Rachel considered the similarity of her situation. What was so different about her mother marrying out of need from what she had just done herself?

She thought of the price her parents had paid, and knew it to be too much.

Damon came in then, and she looked up at him, startled. Her husband.

And yet in his face right now she saw not the Damon she knew—the one who juggled in restaurants and laughed with her baby and looked at her with such unguarded tenderness—but a remote stranger.

He sat down and looked at her gravely.

"Please don't tell me anything else is wrong," she implored him.

"Actually, something is right."

"I need some good news."

"I thought you might. Phillip opened this by accident." He passed her the letter from the children's publisher.

She looked at him, and then down at the letter. She scanned it briefly, and then unsure she had read it properly, she read it again. She felt a wondrous blossoming of joy inside her, and she looked up at him and smiled and wanted to throw her arms around him and wanted him to pick her up and whirl her around the room.

"Does this say I've sold a book?" she asked.

"It does," he said, and he looked as though he was trying to be happy but could not find it in himself.

"Damon, what's wrong? You haven't heard something of Victoria, have you?"

"Of course not. I would tell you. Nothing's wrong." But he was looking at her as if he was memorizing her features. As if some part of him was saying goodbye. That feeling of dread came back. A certainty, learned in that bleak childhood, that good things did not and could not last.

"Rachel, I think we've made a mistake. No, not we. Me. I've made a mistake."

She sat perfectly still. Hadn't she known from the first this moment would come? She just hadn't expected that he would know so soon that she was not suitable. Of course she was not suitable. Any minute her father was probably going to be unmasked as the most notorious kidnapper in Thortonburg's history. A man who had kidnapped the woman he had raised as his own daughter.

Damon could have married a princess or a duchess or a lady, and his mother had probably let him know that. A woman whose history, when exposed to the glaring light of the press, was not going to include a lift operator at a ski resort in Canada who liked to smoke things that smelled funny.

She refused to let him see the effect his words were having on her. She tilted her chin up at him, and swung her hair back over her shoulder in a gesture she hoped showed a nonchalance that hid the breaking of a heart.

How could her heart be breaking? She barely knew this man.

And yet even as she tried to tell herself that, she thought of the first time she had seen him, coming up the steps of the police station, how he had gone to that poor, wretched man and offered comfort to him. She thought of him vacuuming her floor and playing with her baby, and juggling water glasses, and building sand castles.

Maybe she did not know *things* about him. She did not know where he had gone to school, or what business interests filled his days. She did not know if he played chess or if he liked fine art and brandy.

Those things took some time to find out.

But this thing about his heart, she knew. She had known

instantly who he was. She had known his soul, and the goodness of it from their first moments.

She, who had known so little goodness, had been drawn to him like a woman who had crossed the desert, and who was parched to near death, and he was the spring.

"Rachel, I've been so unfair to you."

She dared not speak.

He was looking away, unfocused, staring at her sleeping baby.

"I was selfish beyond measure, and for that I apologize."

She said nothing, looking down at the photo album in her lap as though some answer would suddenly appear on it that told her what to do, as though some magical solution might appear that could keep this catastrophe from unfolding.

"Rachel, I thought you needed me." He nodded at the letter. "I have insulted you by insinuating that you needed me to look after you, that I could give you more than you could somehow give yourself. I was wrong."

The words sounded so lovely, how could they be hurting so much? Of course, this would have been part of his royal training, too. How to remove himself from awkward situations with grace. Pizzazz, even.

"I want you to stay here as long as you want to," he said gently. "At least until Victoria is found and safe. And then I'm giving you the cottage. You and Carly."

For a wild moment she held tight to that thread of hope. She would still see him, they would live on the same island. Their paths would still cross. Maybe they would have time to learn those things about each other that they did not know.

Small things such as did he like dogs? Big ones or small ones? Did he like to have a cat on his lap and sit in front of a fire in the dreary days of winter? Did he spend hot summer days on his boat, or by the pool? In the spring did he ever wear a sprig of some fresh flower in his lapel? Did he watch television? What programs made him laugh? Did he like opera or rock music? How did he eat his steak? Rare or well?

All those questions had seemed unimportant to her, until just now, when she realized she might never know the answers.

Because, of course, she could not accept the cottage as a gift. It was far too extravagant. Her pride would never allow her to accept it, a kind brush-off, complete with a house.

"Rachel, I saw you as solving a problem for me, and me solving one for you, but that—" he nodded at the letter "—I think that means all your problems are solved."

Never mind the broken heart, she thought with faint bitterness, and then thought of the truth of that.

She loved him.

She did not know precisely when it had happened, or where. Maybe in those first few moments, but she loved him, and he was right, if for the wrong reasons. It would be better that it ended now, for she sensed within herself that this love she felt for him would grow and grow and grow. And what would happen to her when it was not reciprocated?

Would she become what her mother had been: weak, desperate for his love and approval?

Would he become what her father had become? A man bitter that he had thrown away his chance for genuine happiness to become a meal ticket, a provider, a function, rather than a human being?

No, he was right. To end it sooner would be better than later.

"Rachel, I thought I was giving you a way out, but really I was bringing you in. Remember once you called my world a prison? I thought today what kind of man invites a woman to share the cell with him? I thought of you being hounded by the press, and later Carly, and I felt like I had done you a grave disservice."

And of course the press would hound her once everything came out about her father, and her sister. She did not want to bring him disgrace.

She could hear his voice going on, his words smooth and sincere if somehow weary, but she really couldn't catch their meaning. It was taking all her energy now to keep her composure, to smile at him as though she understood, to not fall apart.

Even so, the photo album fell from her nerveless fingers, and she looked at it and wanted to laugh hysterically.

She had dropped the teacup when he had asked her to marry him, and now the photo album when he was telling her he wanted to get unmarried after a single day.

A day she had thought was rather splendid, playing in the sunshine with him and her baby. The kind of day that she had looked greedily forward to repeating again and again.

As if he didn't have other things to do besides entertain her and her daughter. Important things.

He reached for the album. It had opened on a page, and he pulled it onto his lap and scowled thoughtfully at it.

"Rachel," he finally said, "you'd better look at this picture."

She looked at the picture. "Oh," she said brightly. "It's always been one of my favorites. It was taken years ago, when Ginger was just young. Father fancied she was going to be a hunting dog. And there she is, snoozing in the sun, as the pheasant walks by. I always thought he should enter it in a contest. It's so charming.'' She babbled, trying so hard to be bright and light.

''Rachel, look at the background of the picture,'' he said softly.

She gave him a confused look, and then did what he asked. She gasped. The dog was on the front porch of a cabin made of rough logs. In the background, mounted on the logs, was an old rifle.

She looked up at him. She got up and went over to where she had set the envelope from Lance and took out the pictures. They studied them together, comparing.

There was no doubt.

''That's where your sister is,'' he said, and his hand covered hers.

And then they were doing exactly what she had hoped would happen they would do when they found out about her book contract.

He picked her up by the waist and lifted her in the air, and shouted with exuberance, ''That's where Victoria is!''

And they laughed together until she thought her heart would run over with the pure joy of sharing laughter with him. Bittersweet. How she wished she could make this moment last forever.

And maybe she could. By memorizing it, maybe she could return to this place again and again in her mind. When the days seemed too bleak and lonely, when the winter seemed too cold, she could come back here, to this place in her heart that would glow forever warm with remembrance.

''I'd forgotten all about that place,'' she said, when he finally set her down. ''It's a hunting lodge that belonged to my father's uncle. I'd forgotten all about it.''

"But you know where it is?"

"Yes. Yes, I know where it is."

"I'm calling Grayson right now."

She took a deep breath. She wanted nothing more than for her sister to be found. Even though it meant what she shared with Damon would be over.

He had said he was going to set her free.

How ironic that she knew she would never feel truly free again. A part of her now would always look back with yearning, with aching, with wistfulness, on these few magic days when she had been allowed to be the princess in a fairy tale.

Damon watched her carefully when he told her his decision. He longed to see something in her face that said that was not how she wished it to be, but nothing showed.

She knew, then, as well as he, that the letter changed everything.

"Yes, I'll call Grayson now," he repeated quietly to Rachel. The phone was by the window and when he looked out it, he could see that the sun was going down. He yanked the curtain cord, and the drapes closed with a swish.

"Grayson, please. Damon Montague." He turned and looked at Rachel.

Her face seemed very white, but when she saw him looking she smiled.

As if it didn't matter to her in the least that their marriage was over before it had really begun.

He told himself to stop being so self-centered. They were one step closer to finding her sister. She was entitled to be happy about that.

Lance Grayson came on the line.

"Rachel has found a photograph in an old family album. The background of it matches the one you sent over this afternoon. Yes. I'll put her on.''

She came to the phone. He watched her cross the floor, marveling at her grace and her beauty. He could bear to be with her no longer without answering the cry in his heart that wanted him to beg her.

To love him.

To stay.

To share his life with him in every way.

He handed her the phone, touched her cheek, a lingering touch, the touch of a man trying to memorize the softness of her skin for all time, and then he turned on his heel and left the room, closing the door quietly behind him.

Chapter Ten

After Rachel hung up from speaking to Lance Grayson, she found herself marveling at the strength of the man, the confidence he was able to instill in her, even over the telephone. She felt as though he was a man who was not easily excited and yet she knew she had heard contained excitement in his voice when she had told him about the lodge and where it was.

He was going to find Victoria.

She knew it with her whole heart and soul.

Damon had left her bedroom, and she went and peeked through the door into his, but it was also empty.

She wandered back into hers, checked Carly, then looked at the boxes from the dress store still stacked neatly in the corner.

Most of them would never be opened now.

Absently she went over and plucked the box off the top and opened it. She frowned. She had never tried on anything that looked like this.

She took the garment out of the tissue paper and stared at it.

It was beautiful, pure white and lacy, a negligee, with a matching jacket.

It was like nothing she had ever owned before, and while part of her urged her, sternly, to put it back in the box, another part of her urged her, strongly, to put it on.

Where had it come from? Damon must have bought it for her. She listened to the second voice, and dropping her clothes to the floor, slipped the negligee over her naked flesh.

It felt exquisite, soft and silky and sexy.

She looked at her reflection in the floor-length mirror behind her door and gasped softly. She looked like a bride in every sense of the word. Why would Damon have bought something so sensual for her when he had known their marriage would never have this element to it? She took off the jacket and set it carefully on the chair beside the bed, then crawled under the covers.

But after tossing and turning for a restless hour, waiting to hear Damon come in, she got up and put on the jacket. She felt exquisite as she moved, as though she was graceful and beautiful and every bit a princess trailing the yards of film and gossamer behind her as she went out into the quiet apartment.

On her rather rushed tour of Damon's quarters, she had noticed they included a small kitchen that looked as if it had never been used, but she still hoped maybe she could find a glass of milk and a microwave there.

It was very quiet, the moon streaming through large windows. She didn't need to turn on a light. And then she saw a door, which had always been firmly closed, was slightly ajar and heard a sound from within. She went over to it, and pushed the door open a little more.

The room was a nursery. The moonlight came through the lace-framed windows, and she could see what a beautiful room it was. Sunshine-yellow, a huge Pooh painted on one wall. And Damon sitting in the rocker. That was the sound she had heard, then, the rocker going back and forth, creaking.

Listening to some command of her heart, she stepped into the room.

Damon could not believe how beautiful she looked as she came through the doorway. He remembered now seeing the outfit she wore on a rack in the store that day, and asking Rosalitta to send it, a surprise. But the surprise was on him, for gone was her schoolgirl innocence. She looked ravishing.

He had come here to think. To feel.

And he had thought what he would feel was a great sadness at what he had told her tonight. But instead, he had felt the oddest sense of tranquility. Sorry, with all his heart and beyond, that he could not keep her, but content with himself. He had done the right thing by letting her go.

The loving thing.

Because, it had come to him in the dark quiet of this room, that real love would always want what was highest and best for the other person. Real love would not put them in a cage, but rather would open the cage door and say, "Fly."

How had he come to genuinely love her in such a short period of time? It was enough, he thought whimsically, to make one ponder ethereal issues. Had he known her in another lifetime? Had his spirit recognized her spirit? Or did he have helpers in heaven now, watching out for him, guiding him down roads he had never journeyed down before?

And if that was so, why was it they could not help love to stay?

Perhaps what they really were helping him do was to find out what kind of man he really was.

And so when she came in and paused in the doorway, he could not help but wonder if she had been brought to him by those helpers, so he could see her looking so lovely, and remember her like this, his princess, always.

He stood up.

"I'm sorry," she said. "I couldn't sleep. I heard something in here. I'll go."

"No, don't go." He held out his hands to her, and she came, seeming to float across the floor, a heavenly presence. And was that not what love was, after all? A way that heaven made itself known in the humble home of a man's heart?

She came and took his hands, gazed up at him, her eyes wide, shimmering green. "This is obviously a very private place for you."

Yes. But suddenly it seemed there was no part of himself that he wanted to keep private from her.

"It's all right," he said, and found he meant it.

"It's a beautiful room," she said. "I love Pooh."

"Sharon painted him. Right down to the bumblebee on his nose." He laughed softly, remembering.

"Is there anything you regret, Damon?" she whispered, and the way her eyes held his made him feel as though words should be unnecessary. Could she not see his soul?

"I regret I didn't tell her more often what she meant to me."

Rachel nodded. "That is my same regret, with Victoria."

"You'll have an opportunity to tell her that."

"I think it is another opportunity I have been given." She looked away from him, took a deep breath and looked back. "I've been thinking of the things you said to me tonight. About this marriage being about you being selfish. I want you to know how wrong you are."

"I'm not wrong."

"Damon, don't make me leave here full of regrets for the things I did not say, the way I feel with my sister."

He was silent, because he could see something tortured in her eyes.

"You may think that you were selfish, but I saw you in a different light. I saw you—and see you—as the most altruistic man I have ever known."

He started to protest, but she held up her hand firmly.

"This has been the most difficult time of my life, with my sister missing, and knowing my father is most likely behind it, and finding out my family was one gigantic sham."

She released his hands, turned from him, walked to the window and gazed out. "And yet, there are threads of joy wound all through this time. You. You were my joy. You looked after me and made me feel cared about in a way I never have been in my life. At a time when I thought I was so weak, you showed me something at my very core. Strength."

She turned and faced him again. "So I have to be strong enough to say this to you." She took a deep shuddering breath. "I may never have an opportunity to be honest with you again, Damon, so I am going to be honest with you now.

"I am tired of being controlled by you. *You* want to be married. *You* want to be unmarried. All these noble speeches about what *you* want for *me*. But have you ever asked me what I want for myself?''

He felt his mouth drop open. He had seen her softness, always, but her fire was intoxicating.

''Why haven't you asked me that?'' she demanded. ''Do I strike you as such a fool that I wouldn't even know what I want for myself?''

''Rachel, of course not.''

''Then ask me!''

''Rachel,'' he said obediently, watching in awe as she showed him her full power and grace and glory, ''what do you want for yourself?''

''I want what all ordinary women want, Damon. And believe it or not, that's not a prince. It's love. I told your mother this. I would have married a bricklayer for love.''

''That's exactly what I'm talking about. I'm letting you go, so that you can find your bricklayer, so that you can be happy, so that—''

''It's too late for the bricklayer, Damon. Unless you plan on changing professions anytime soon.''

He went very still.

''I can't leave without telling you this.'' Her face was proud and fierce, but her voice revealed her vulnerability in its tenderness. ''Damon, I love you.''

The shock of it rippled through him, like an electric current spreading a slow warmth everywhere in him that his blood flowed.

''I know,'' she continued, ''it seems impossible, or naive, that I could love you after such a short period of time. But I do. With my whole heart and soul. Like I have never loved before. And I would have loved you no matter what. My soul would have recognized your soul no matter what you did, if you were a bricklayer or a prince.

''I can understand that you want me to go. My father

is about to bring disgrace upon himself and everything he's ever touched—''

He found himself crossing the distance between them, taking her shoulders in his hands. ''Rachel! Don't say that. Your father has nothing to do with this. Nothing! I wanted what was best for you. That's all I ever thought of.''

''That kind of sounds like love to me, Damon.''

''You believe me, don't you?''

''Yes,'' she whispered, and then said again, bravely, fiercely, ''I love you.''

He could not believe what he was hearing. What he was seeing in her eyes. Oh, Lord, it was as if his whole life had been leading to this moment.

He gathered her in his arms, and he kissed the top of her head, and her earlobes, and her neck, and the lovely V above that negligee. And he whispered, from the bottom of his soul, ''I love you, too.''

She pulled back from him and stared at him, scanning his face. ''Do you mean that?''

He laughed, a good sound, a sound that mirrored the singing in his heart. ''With my whole heart and soul.''

And then she was kissing him, his eyes and his lips and his cheeks, raining frantic kisses on him, as though she could never get enough.

He pulled away from her. It took everything he had, but he pulled away from her. He knew what he wanted to give her.

''Go to bed,'' he told her gently.

''I want to go with you,'' she said fiercely.

''No.''

She looked as if she would crumple in front of him, and so he gathered her in his arms one last time and kissed her. Passionately. A kiss that put every single thing he was feeling into it.

When he was done, he once again put her away from him, knowing she knew now exactly what he felt. "Go to bed," he told her firmly.

And with one last bewildered look she turned from him, gathered the long gossamer folds of the negligee and ran from the room.

He thought he had a great deal to do, and very little time to do it in.

She went back to her bed, and climbed into it. He had said he loved her, but he had sent her away again. Warm milk was now the furthest thing from her mind. Warm skin, his, and the way it had felt beneath her fingertips made her want to cry out with yearning.

She closed her eyes, thinking she would feel confused and unable to sleep. But she didn't. She wrapped her arms around her pillow and let her inner voice speak to her of truth. The truth as it had been in his eyes and his lips tonight. She had found the oasis in the desert that she had searched for her entire life. Not a mirage this time. The oasis was love.

She awoke to a gentle shaking of her shoulder. The night melted dreamlike, as if it had never been, into the first pink streaks of dawn.

"Princess, wake up."

It must be a dream, of course, because no one knew she was a princess. Rachel struggled to open her eyes. Light was streaming through her window, and Carly was sitting on Bonnie's hip.

"What?" she said, struggling to sit up. "What?"

"Prince Damon requests the honor of your presence,"

Bonnie said, smiling ear to ear. "Oh, I can't believe it. It's so romantic."

"Bonnie, what is romantic?"

"He's waiting by the front stairs for you. Can you find your way to the main staircase, or shall I help you?"

She knew she could find him. She scrambled out of bed. "I need to get dressed, I need to—"

But Bonnie was holding out the filmy jacket of the negligee for her. "Just go."

"Like this?"

"Exactly like that."

Rachel pulled the jacket over the negligee, and went, barefoot, down the hallways and stairs, past servants, all of whom seemed to be smiling as though they knew the most delightful secret.

Finally, she came to the bottom of the main staircase. Damon was not there, but the front door of the castle was open. She went outside.

Damon was sitting there on the most beautiful horse— a knight, a prince, a man who had crossed the desert.

She froze on the stone landing, and looked down at him. She saw the curtains twitching at nearly every window. "Damon, what is it? The whole house is watching and I'm out here in my nightdress!"

"I'm taking a lesson from Roland. I'm declaring myself in no uncertain terms. I don't want you to look back on our relationship and regret all the moments it didn't have, the moments I didn't give you."

"Damon, get down off that horse, and come in the house."

"No. I want you to have high romance. A bold statement of love declaring itself. Giddy madness." He held out his hand to her.

"I can't go racing across the countryside on horseback with you in my nightgown, Damon!"

"Why on earth not?"

She pondered that for a moment, and then wondered *why on earth not?* She had always been so correct. He was inviting her to share the adventure with him. The full, fantastic adventure of being in love, of journeying into the magnificent mystery of the human heart.

Slowly, she went down the steps, and then stood beside the magnificent animal he rode, gazing up at him. She put her hand in his.

He kicked his foot out of the stirrup. She put her foot in the stirrup, and found herself swung up on the horse behind him, the long, white negligee spread over the horse's hindquarters.

She wrapped her arms tight around Damon's waist and buried her nose in his shoulder. She marveled at the scent of him, the strength.

"Hang on tight," he told her.

She did not think she could hang on any tighter. And then they were galloping out of the drive, turning west into a meadow and then heading up into the lush greenness of the hills.

She shouted with exuberance, a feeling of pure freedom enveloping her as they galloped along, the wind in their faces and hair.

After a while he slowed the horse to a sedate walk, steering the horse ever upward, seeming to have an exact destination in mind.

They came to the cottage, Cliff Croft. He helped her down and then slid gracefully off the horse himself. He tied the horse to a tree, and took her arm in his.

The cottage looked different. She realized the grounds had been carefully manicured, and pots of spring flowers lined the walks. She could see drapes had been hung at the windows.

"This is where we are going to live," he told her. "You and me and Carly. And I hope one day a brother or a sister for Carly."

And then he picked her up, swung her into his arms and kissed her nose. When he looked into her face, he sighed with great happiness. "I have dreamed of this moment," he said, and he walked up to the door and nudged it with his toe, "when you would gaze at me with a look of excitement and anticipation in your eyes that would turn my blood to fire."

He carried her over the threshold.

She was stunned by the interior of the cottage. It had been completely furnished. He set her down, and smiled as she looked into the living room, furnished now with the plump blue checked sofas out of the furniture shop in Thortonburg. There were the wing chairs and the chest.

"Where's the dog by the fire?" she teased him, and then heard a whine from the kitchen. "Damon!"

"For Carly."

"How did you do all this?"

"Every now and then being a prince has some distinct perks."

He gave her a tour of the house, the lovely kitchen done in blues and whites, a little golden retriever puppy whining behind a gate on the back porch. Carly's room done in primary colors and overflowing with stuffed animals and toys.

And then, of course, the master bedroom.

She gasped with delight when she saw it. The huge four-poster bed dominated the design, white pillows mounded on the lacy cover.

It was a bedroom straight out of a fairy tale.

She turned and looked at him, this generous, gorgeous, good-hearted man who was her husband.

And suddenly nothing else mattered except him. She went into his waiting arms. He held her, and then his lips found her lips.

"Wait, there's one more thing." He slipped the ring from his pocket. "I'm ready to tell the whole world you are my wife."

"The instant they find Victoria," she agreed as he slipped the band of thick yellow gold onto her finger.

She wrapped her arms around the strong column of his neck, and pulled his lips down to her own, hungry for him.

Then they were on the bed, and the sun was streaming in the windows across the broadness of his shoulders, and she let her fingers explore the texture of his skin with quiet reverence.

She hesitated only a moment, and then undid the buttons on his shirt, slipped her hand inside, closed her eyes and savored the feel of him, warm silken skin stretched over the hard, mounded muscles of his chest. Lightly, with her fingertips, she explored the wideness of his shoulder, the deepness of his chest, the ridges of his ribs, the hard plane of his stomach.

She opened her eyes, and looked into his, darkened with feverish wanting. She slipped the shirt from his shoulders, and let her lips go where her hand had gone before, tasting him.

With a savage groan, he reversed their positions, and she found herself pinned beneath him, looking up into his eyes, the tenderness overlaid now with heat so intense she could feel everything within her that might have held back—any shyness, any reserve, any inhibition—evaporate.

The negligee jacket went first, his hands sure, his gaze

never wavering from her face. And then he touched her. Softly. Reverently. A brush of fingertips, followed by the brush of his lips. She arched against him, and his hands pinned her as his tongue found her heart and painted a sensuous circle around it, an ever-widening circle.

"Damon," she said hoarsely, looking at the top of his dark head. "Damon!" she cried as his tongue found yet another soft and secret place of her deepest pleasure.

He teased and tormented her with his hands and his mouth and his tongue, until she was nearly sobbing with wanting that highest expression of love fulfilling itself between a man and a woman. His eyes, smoky with desire, brimming with an intensity of love she could barely comprehend, beckoned her to follow him to new heights, to go beyond where she had ever gone before, to throw herself into the adventure of being a woman and a man together.

Finally, in rippling explosions that spiraled higher and higher until she soared with eagles and danced with clouds, they became as one.

A long time later they lay in the circle of each other's arms, the morning sunlight washing over them.

"I feel," she said, "as if I was a virgin, as if I had never given myself to anyone before, as if I held back what was most special about me for you."

"That's exactly how I feel," he said softly. "Exactly."

In that moment she felt no fear, only a great certainty that all of life unfolds as it should, that events were interrelated in ways that the human mind was only occasionally allowed to grasp—bad leading to good, suffering leading to miracles, in the end the plan being one of such glory, a heart could barely hold it.

She sensed, deep in that heart, that Victoria would be rescued and that *her* miracle was about to begin....

*   *   *   *   *

Turn the page
for a sneak preview of

A ROYAL MISSION

by beloved author
Elizabeth August,

on sale in Silhouette Romance
in May 2000.

As ROYALLY WED concludes,
the skeleton in the Thortons' closet
is finally put to rest!

Using only the full moon to light his way, Lance Grayson moved stealthily through the woods. His destination was the one-room log cabin ahead. Its porch roof sagged in one corner and its windows were boarded up. Weeds, underbrush and small trees were reclaiming the clearing in which it sat. Pausing, he used night vision binoculars to survey the scene in front of him. The place looked totally abandoned. Silently, Lance cursed. Time was running short to find Victoria Rockford, and it looked as if this lead was a dud.

Even worse, it was his only lead.

He turned the binoculars to the woods surrounding the cabin. His best men were minding the perimeter. In a lowered voice he spoke into the headphone, calling each man by name. Each responded with, "In position, sir."

The image of Victoria Rockford haunted him. In the pictures he'd seen, she looked so alive, so vital. That she could die because he did not find her in time tore at his very soul. It bothered him that this assignment seemed more personal, more urgent. He was normally much cooler, much more detached.

"Hold your positions," he said. "Looks like a wild-goose chase, but I'm going to take a closer look."

Making his way to a side window, he looked in through one of the spaces between the boards. With only slender rays of moonlight making their way into the interior, he could see very little. He was lifting the night vision binoculars to his eyes when he heard it…a soft moan. Peering through the binoculars, he allowed triumph to flow through him. On a bed in a far corner lay a woman, her hands shackled to the brass headrail, her feet bound to the footrail with rope.

"Looks like this might not have been a wild-goose chase, after all."

Victoria Rockford fought the drugs she'd been given to sedate her and tried to focus her thoughts. Her struggle proved futile. Her mind remained foggy and the temptation to give in to sleep grew stronger. Her movements slow and weak, she closed her hands around the brass poles of the headboard and gave a jerk on the rope that bound her feet. She'd done this a hundred times before. Each time she hoped the bed would finally give way, crumble to pieces and allow her to escape.

It didn't.

She wanted to scream in frustration, but the gag in her mouth prevented that. Mentally, she cursed "The Whisperer," the name she'd dubbed her kidnapper, and vowed vengeance should she ever get free.

When she got free, she corrected herself, refusing to consider the alternative.

Hearing a footfall on the porch, she froze. An adrenaline rush brought some clarity to her sluggish mind. Her captor came twice a day to feed her and to allow her to use the facilities. Blindfolded so that she could not tell if it was day or night, her sense of time had been severely affected. Still, she was certain it was too soon for her captor to be returning. Normally by the time he came, the drugs had worn off enough that she had more coordination. Had the time come to find out why she'd been kidnapped?

Fear threatened to overwhelm her. Her jaw clenched. If this was "The Whisperer" come back early, she would not go down without a fight.

Lance's gaze traveled over the woman on the bed. Shining his flashlight on her, he confirmed he'd found the grand duke's daughter. Her long dark hair was in a mass of disarray, framing a face that was a strikingly beautiful version of the Thorton features.

"Miss Rockford, I'm Lance Grayson, head of the Royal Security Detail of Thortonburg," he said, flipping off the light before working her blindfold loose. If her kidnapper came back, Lance didn't want him to spot a light in the cabin and scare him off before his men could nab him.

Removing the gag, Lance tossed it aside. Next he removed a small kit of lock-picking tools to unfasten the handcuffs. While he worked, he checked in with his men. The perimeter was secure and no one was approaching. He ordered his jeep brought to the front of the cabin for transport.

Having freed her hands, Lance took out his knife and cut the bonds holding her feet. "Can you sit up?" he asked, easing her into an upright position.

"I don't feel so good," she murmured, her hands fastening around his upper arms for support.

An intense surge of protectiveness swept through

Lance. Along with the desire to throttle the men who had done this to her.

"You're going to be fine," he assured her as he scooped her into his arms. "I'll see to that...."

VIRGIN BRIDES

Join
Silhouette Romance
as the New Year brings new
virgin brides down the aisle!

On Sale December 1999
THE BRIDAL BARGAIN
by Stella Bagwell (SR #1414)

On Sale February 2000
WAITING FOR THE WEDDING
by Carla Cassidy (SR #1426)

On Sale April 2000
HIS WILD YOUNG BRIDE
by Donna Clayton (SR #1441)

Watch for more **Virgin Brides** stories from
your favorite authors later in 2000!

VIRGIN BRIDES
only from

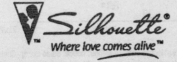

Silhouette®
Where love comes alive™

Available at your favorite retail outlet.

Visit us at www.romance.net

SRVB00

If you enjoyed what you just read,
then we've got an offer you can't resist!

Take 2 bestselling love stories FREE!

Plus get a FREE surprise gift!

Clip this page and mail it to Silhouette Reader Service™

IN U.S.A.	IN CANADA
3010 Walden Ave.	P.O. Box 609
P.O. Box 1867	Fort Erie, Ontario
Buffalo, N.Y. 14240-1867	L2A 5X3

YES! Please send me 2 free Silhouette Romance® novels and my free surprise gift. Then send me 6 brand-new novels every month, which I will receive months before they're available in stores. In the U.S.A., bill me at the bargain price of $2.90 plus 25¢ delivery per book and applicable sales tax, if any*. In Canada, bill me at the bargain price of $3.25 plus 25¢ delivery per book and applicable taxes**. That's the complete price and a savings of at least 10% off the cover prices—what a great deal! I understand that accepting the 2 free books and gift places me under no obligation ever to buy any books. I can always return a shipment and cancel at any time. Even if I never buy another book from Silhouette, the 2 free books and gift are mine to keep forever. So why not take us up on our invitation. You'll be glad you did!

215 SEN C24Q
315 SEN C24R

Name	(PLEASE PRINT)	
Address	Apt.#	
City	State/Prov.	Zip/Postal Code

* Terms and prices subject to change without notice. Sales tax applicable in N.Y.
** Canadian residents will be charged applicable provincial taxes and GST.
  All orders subject to approval. Offer limited to one per household.
  ® are registered trademarks of Harlequin Enterprises Limited.

SROM00_R   ©1998 Harlequin Enterprises Limited

If you enjoyed what you just read,
then we've got an offer you can't resist!

Take 2 bestselling love stories FREE!

Plus get a FREE surprise gift!

Clip this page and mail it to Silhouette Reader Service™

IN U.S.A.	**IN CANADA**
3010 Walden Ave.	P.O. Box 609
P.O. Box 1867	Fort Erie, Ontario
Buffalo, N.Y. 14240-1867	L2A 5X3

YES! Please send me 2 free Silhouette Romance® novels and my free surprise gift. Then send me 6 brand-new novels every month, which I will receive months before they're available in stores. In the U.S.A., bill me at the bargain price of $2.90 plus 25¢ delivery per book and applicable sales tax, if any*. In Canada, bill me at the bargain price of $3.25 plus 25¢ delivery per book and applicable taxes**. That's the complete price and a savings of at least 10% off the cover prices—what a great deal! I understand that accepting the 2 free books and gift places me under no obligation ever to buy any books. I can always return a shipment and cancel at any time. Even if I never buy another book from Silhouette, the 2 free books and gift are mine to keep forever. So why not take us up on our invitation. You'll be glad you did!

215 SEN C24Q
315 SEN C24R

Name	(PLEASE PRINT)	
Address	Apt.#	
City	State/Prov.	Zip/Postal Code

* Terms and prices subject to change without notice. Sales tax applicable in N.Y.
** Canadian residents will be charged applicable provincial taxes and GST.
All orders subject to approval. Offer limited to one per household.
® are registered trademarks of Harlequin Enterprises Limited.

SROM00_R   ©1998 Harlequin Enterprises Limited

Look Who's Celebrating Our 20th Anniversary:

"Happy 20th birthday, Silhouette. You made the writing dream of hundreds of women a reality. You enabled us to give [women] the stories [they] wanted to read and helped us teach [them] about the power of love."

—*New York Times* bestselling author
Debbie Macomber

"I wish you continued success, Silhouette Books.... Thank you for giving me a chance to do what I love best in all the world."

—International bestselling author
Diana Palmer

"A visit to Silhouette is a guaranteed happy ending, a chance to touch magic for a little while.... It refreshes and revitalizes and makes us feel better.... I hope Silhouette goes on forever."

—Award-winning bestselling author
Marie Ferrarella

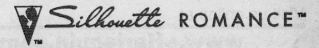

SILHOUETTE'S 20TH ANNIVERSARY CONTEST
OFFICIAL RULES
NO PURCHASE NECESSARY TO ENTER

1. To enter, follow directions published in the offer to which you are responding. Contest begins 1/1/00 and ends on 8/24/00 (the "Promotion Period"). Method of entry may vary. Mailed entries must be postmarked by 8/24/00, and received by 8/31/00.

2. During the Promotion Period, the Contest may be presented via the Internet. Entry via the Internet may be restricted to residents of certain geographic areas that are disclosed on the Web site. To enter via the Internet, if you are a resident of a geographic area in which Internet entry is permissible, follow the directions displayed on-line, including typing your essay of 100 words or fewer telling us "Where In The World Your Love Will Come Alive." On-line entries must be received by 11:59 p.m. Eastern Standard time on 8/24/00. Limit one e-mail entry per person, household and e-mail address per day, per presentation. If you are a resident of a geographic area in which entry via the Internet is permissible, you may, in lieu of submitting an entry on-line, enter by mail, by hand-printing your name, address, telephone number and contest number/name on an 8"x 11" plain piece of paper and telling us in 100 words or fewer "Where In The World Your Love Will Come Alive," and mailing via first-class mail to: Silhouette 20th Anniversary Contest, (in the U.S.) P.O. Box 9069, Buffalo, NY 14269-9069; (In Canada) P.O. Box 637, Fort Erie, Ontario, Canada L2A 5X3. Limit one 8"x 11" mailed entry per person, household and e-mail address per day. On-line and/or 8"x 11" mailed entries received from persons residing in geographic areas in which Internet entry is not permissible will be disqualified. No liability is assumed for lost, late, incomplete, inaccurate, nondelivered or misdirected mail, or misdirected e-mail, for technical, hardware or software failures of any kind, lost or unavailable network connection, or failed, incomplete, garbled or delayed computer transmission or any human error which may occur in the receipt or processing of the entries in the contest.

3. Essays will be judged by a panel of members of the Silhouette editorial and marketing staff based on the following criteria:

   > Sincerity (believability, credibility)—50%
   > Originality (freshness, creativity)—30%
   > Aptness (appropriateness to contest ideas)—20%

   Purchase or acceptance of a product offer does not improve your chances of winning. In the event of a tie, duplicate prizes will be awarded.

4. All entries become the property of Harlequin Enterprises Ltd., and will not be returned. Winner will be determined no later than 10/31/00 and will be notified by mail. Grand Prize winner will be required to sign and return Affidavit of Eligibility within 15 days of receipt of notification. Noncompliance within the time period may result in disqualification and an alternative winner may be selected. All municipal, provincial, federal, state and local laws and regulations apply. Contest open only to residents of the U.S. and Canada who are 18 years of age or older, and is void where prohibited by law. Internet entry is restricted solely to residents of those geographical areas in which Internet entry is permissible. Employees of Torstar Corp., their affiliates, agents and members of their immediate families are not eligible. Taxes on the prizes are the sole responsibility of winners. Entry and acceptance of any prize offered constitutes permission to use winner's name, photograph or other likeness for the purposes of advertising, trade and promotion on behalf of Torstar Corp. without further compensation to the winner, unless prohibited by law. Torstar Corp and D.L. Blair, Inc., their parents, affiliates and subsidiaries, are not responsible for errors in printing or electronic presentation of contest or entries. In the event of printing or other errors which may result in unintended prize values or duplication of prizes, all affected contest materials or entries shall be null and void. If for any reason the Internet portion of the contest is not capable of running as planned, including infection by computer virus, bugs, tampering, unauthorized intervention, fraud, technical failures, or any other causes beyond the control of Torstar Corp. which corrupt or affect the administration, secrecy, fairness, integrity or proper conduct of the contest, Torstar Corp. reserves the right, at its sole discretion, to disqualify any individual who tampers with the entry process and to cancel, terminate, modify or suspend the contest or the Internet portion thereof. In the event of a dispute regarding an on-line entry, the entry will be deemed submitted by the authorized holder of the e-mail account submitted at the time of entry. Authorized account holder is defined as the natural person who is assigned to an e-mail address by an Internet access provider, on-line service provider or other organization that is responsible for arranging e-mail address for the domain associated with the submitted e-mail address.

5. Prizes: Grand Prize—a $10,000 vacation to anywhere in the world. Travelers (at least one must be 18 years of age or older) or parent or guardian if one traveler is a minor, must sign and return a Release of Liability prior to departure. Travel must be completed by December 31, 2001, and is subject to space and accommodations availability. Two hundred (200) Second Prizes—a two-book limited edition autographed collector set from one of the Silhouette Anniversary authors: Nora Roberts, Diana Palmer, Linda Howard or Annette Broadrick (value $10.00 each set). All prizes are valued in U.S. dollars.

6. For a list of winners (available after 10/31/00), send a self-addressed, stamped envelope to: Harlequin Silhouette 20th Anniversary Winners, P.O. Box 4200, Blair, NE 68009-4200.

Contest sponsored by Torstar Corp., P.O. Box 9042, Buffalo, NY 14269-9042.

PS20RULES

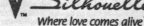
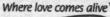